i believe

i believe you live once and that better opportunities are lost on second chances.
i believe true love is about as real as Santa Claus, but 'tis the season, so let's play this game...
i believe that you fall in "love" with the person who lets you love him or her the way you want, on your terms.
i believe if someone says he "loves" you more than air, he's lying to you.
i believe that "love" is not about forgiveness, it's about acceptance, and acceptance keeps relationships alive.
i believe in the stories that are never told.
i believe that if you have to "fight" for love, you're trying to force a square peg into a round hole.
i believe that your flaws are what make you beautiful. Deal with it.
i believe that two people are just that - two people.
i believe that two married people are two individuals with one shared goal and one shared delusion.
i believe delusions are a good thing until you start getting drugs, threesomes and whips involved. Stay pure.
i believe that in your heart, you have blood not love, and that blood is to the heart what ideas (not love) are to the mind.
i believe that happy endings happen in real life when I fall asleep, thinking of my children's smiles.
i believe that all stories are written for me - that same story means something different for you, and that's okay.
i believe in freedom for everyone; everyone has the right to hunt or to hide or both.
i believe that mothers are sacred and anyone who tells a mother what to do has self-esteem issues.
i believe that true character gets revealed in actions, not in what someone says about him or herself.
i believe that promises are one word, and any one word means nothing.
i believe that if you never hurt, you never find happiness; the bigger you hurt, the bigger your happiness.
i believe in friendships that last a lifetime and in friends that support you even when you are dead wrong.
i believe that most of the decisions you make are the wrong ones. Celebrate your victories. Celebrate hard.
i believe that if you can make decisions objectively, you will never be wrong. Or hurt. Or happy.
i believe that we cry for ourselves, not for others.
i believe that tears are a lot like rage - you need to get that poison out of your system periodically or it will kill you.
i believe that when you die, you die alone, and
i believe that goodbyes are forever.

MORGAN
PARKER

SICK DAY

a novel by

MORGAN PARKER

ISBN 978-0991764846

Follow Morgan Parker on Facebook

Novels by Morgan Parker

Sick Day

Hope

Non Friction

Textual Encounters: 2

Textual Encounters: The Christine + Jake Affair

Coming Soon:

Textual Encounters III

PROLOGUE

Our Story

My bed at the Drake Hotel was big enough for both of us. We kicked our shoes off at the door and went straight to that bed.

I jumped onto the mattress first, my feet landing where the pillows were and my head settling at the foot. I patted the space next to me, where I wanted Oliver to lie.

He complied with the same lame-ass, high-jump leap I had just attempted, but the mattress was so firm that we didn't bounce at all, even as his 180-pound frame dropped next to me. He grunted, then edged closer to me. So close that his face was only a couple of inches from mine, a closeness that, judging by the blotchiness on his face, made him more uncomfortable than it made me.

I laughed at that discomfort.

"You're supposed to sleep on this thing?" he asked.

I giggled like a schoolgirl because that was exactly how he made me feel. The fluttering in my stomach, the impending collapse of my legs earlier when he had laced his hand into mine while we strolled along Michigan Avenue after dinner. My hunger for his lips against mine, against me, all of me, every inch. Yes, like a schoolgirl. And not just because of the physical impression he was leaving on me.

I covered my crooked giggles with my hand, and his eyes didn't seem bothered or even slightly curious about my oversized wedding ring.

This was exactly like a schoolgirl's crush. I had only known Oliver since yesterday afternoon, yet here we lay on my hotel room bed, separated by a couple layers of clothes, our wedding bands, and roughly three inches of tension-infused space.

As my hand moved away from my face, I watched Oliver lick his lips. His pupils dilated as he focused on my mouth.

"What's your favorite color?" he asked, his voice distant. I knew he was lost in me, in the fantasies about what our time in my hotel room could lead to.

"Purple," I said. "Yours?"

"Orange."

I giggled again. This was getting stupid. "Orange is like saying a bus pass is your all-time favoritest car in the whole wide world."

We laughed together. It was getting late. If Oliver was anything like me, he hadn't slept well last night. Our introduction on the plane yesterday—both of us hated flying, and the flight from Vegas had been a choppy one—our flirting in the airport, and then Oliver showing up today at my book signing and press conference, our surprise dinner, our walk, and now this.

At last, I reached out and grabbed his hand. His palm felt clammy, uncertain. I brought it to my chest, placed it above my breast so he wouldn't have to get all nervous and awkward. I *knew* fear was what he felt because that was exactly what I felt, too.

"It's okay, Oliver," I told him. "I know your fears. But sometimes the best decisions are the ones we don't make for ourselves. So I'll make the decisions tonight."

He took a deep breath, opened his mouth to say something, then changed his mind. We stared at each other for what felt like an eternity collapsing with the snap of fingers—a lifetime gone in the blink of an eye.

"Just stay with me tonight and let me memorize every last piece of you."

My name is Olivia Warren, and just because this is my story, it doesn't mean there's a happily ever after at the end of it. I may have made my first night with Oliver Weaver sound prettier than the Holy Gardens at the gates of Heaven. The truth is that *pretty* cannot describe the majority of my relationship with that man.

For starters, the day we met we were both very much married and, to some extent, in love with our respective spouses. I didn't mention that earlier because people generally don't like cheaters. And loving someone, even if you don't fuck them, is indeed cheating—emotional cheating.

That next morning, neither of us woke up because neither of us had fallen asleep in the first place. We rolled out of bed, and Oliver convinced me that today he would show me the city, all of it.

"Why would I want to see all of it?"

He chuckled. "It looks like you just sucked on a lemon! Okay, just the best parts."

"Why?"

He took my hand and pulled me to the door, to our shoes, out to the hall, and to the elevators. We were acting like two kids trapped in the lives of two mid-lifers, struggling with lack of sleep. But we were far too jacked up on the adrenaline-rush of having found our soul mate to slow down and just breathe.

"You'll love this," he promised, and the next thing I remember, we were standing in a vast, all-white room. White floors, windows on two opposite walls. A white table setting with white linens, white side plates, and silver cutlery.

A waiter in a white shirt (and black pants) smiled and gestured for us to sit down. It was the only table in this large white space, but it felt cozy. Oliver made it feel that way.

I leaned forward on the table, my elbows on the edge as I propped my face up to take him in, to take *all* of this experience in. "Where are we?"

"Lunch," he told me. "You're tired, aren't you?"

I nodded and wondered if he had drugged me. As the panic set in, I felt his hand on mine, and a gust of emotion flooded through me. All of this was like something out of a dream sequence in a crazy sci-fi movie. I imagined seeing the finest paintings, the most compelling pieces of art, and I felt the deepest emotion flicker through my head.

When my eyes opened, our lunch had arrived—a nice serving of salmon with a cute salad. The colors of the food were vibrant and alive.

Oliver and I talked about the blurry stuff of reality—our marriages, our kids, our jobs. The disappointment left by each of those things. Oliver paid the bill, and a heartbeat later, I was standing in front of a Monet painting, the train station one. Each stroke of Monet's brush spoke to me in this moment of ultimate fatigue.

"Let's get lost," Oliver said, and we left the Art Institute of Chicago.

The next thing I knew, we were riding a Ferris wheel overlooking Chicago's North and South shores. We walked to the Sears Tower after that, talking shit and laughing and careless. Then we found and sat on the hardest wooden benches in the world—they were at Union Station—and we stared up at the ceiling and got dizzy, as if we were watching the stars at night.

"I need to sleep," I mumbled, my voice whiny and desperate even to my own ears.

We ran through the streets with stupid-big smiles on our faces, all the way back to the Drake, back up to my room, and to the hard bed where we fell asleep holding each other. And somehow—I don't know how—it was love.

Within two days of knowing this wonderful, sweet man, I loved him more than anyone could ever believe possible.

Including Oliver.

But I did, I loved him. Hard and deep, like no human should be allowed to love. The kind of love that destroys you.

PRESENT DAY

CHAPTER 1

5:28 AM

Not a cloud in the sky as the sun rises over the Gold Coast's impressive skyline.

"...couple of minutes before five-thirty on this Friday morning as we ease into the summer's last long weekend," Big C announces as the radio alarm fires off. "So who wants to call in sick and get a head start on what will arguably be one of the finest weekends we've had all year?"

I step away from the floor-to-ceiling windows, noticing Riley's picture on the wall, and smack the alarm's OFF button as I pass the bed on my way to the bathroom. Despite my condo being thirty floors above street level, the hot water arrives almost instantly once I turn on the faucet. It's a nice bathroom—so nice that I feel guilty whenever I use it to, uh, relieve myself. Even standing under the steaming spray from the rainfall showerhead, I feel a little bad about the LeLabo soap pooling on the travertine at my feet. Yes, it's *that* pretty of a bathroom.

So I hurry up, squeegeeing the tile and glass clean before drying my hair and getting dressed.

I love my condo, which explains the OCD cleanliness and near-institutional feel to it. I like it this way, and I probably *should* be institutionalized for what I'm about to do. Grabbing the cordless phone in the kitchen, I drop a Chai Tea Latte K-cup into the Keurig and wait for it to finish brewing before dialing the phone number I know all too well.

It rings five times before the voicemail picks up. If not for the spicy aroma from my girly coffee, I would normally feel slightly ill at the sound of my boss's voice. But the coffee gives me strength; it reminds me of the adventure awaiting me. At the beep, I leave my message, keeping my voice purposely coarse and pained.

"Newman," I groan. "I'm dying. For real this time. I think it's…" I haven't really thought this part through because I've recently become something of an expert at calling in sick, so I blurt the first thing that comes to mind, fully aware that last week's "sickness" was food poisoning: "E-coli poisoning." *Fuck. Tart.* Face-palm fucktart, actually. "Sorry to be doing this to you and the team on a Friday before Labor Day, but…" I cough, then wonder, *Do people cough with e-coli poisoning? Or do they just puke a lot? Or at all?* Whatevs, no point splitting hairs over the details now. "I have to run, Newman. You know where to—" *cough* "—where to find me."

I hang up and laugh because Newman has me against the ropes right now, and that screw-up with the e-coli probably just cost me my job. *Great.*

Grabbing the steaming cup from the Keurig, I head to the Bat Cave—my special name for the den, a tight room with two bean bag chairs and a sixty-inch flat screen that doubles as my gaming and computer screen. All kinds of great ideas are born here. I drop onto red Tipsy (the other chair is called brown Topsy) and hit the remote for the screen.

Once I see that the Japanese Yen has weakened against the US dollar by more than one percent overnight, I turn the television off. And I laugh. Again.

It's not even six o'clock and this beautiful day is already slipping out of my control. I shake my head, take a sip of the Chai Tea Latte, and allow myself to be enveloped by courage. It's exactly what I need if I really plan on writing this text message that kept me up all night.

Grabbing my iPhone, I activate my jAppe messaging service and find the thumbnail of Hope's picture. I tap on her face, a pic that I took just two months ago against her protests. It amazes me that such a small thumbnail can encapsulate the full definition of perfection, but it does. Hope is my perfect.

I type the quick message, and press send. It looks like this:

Me: Let's play sick day together.

Then I watch the iPhone's screen and wait for her to read my message, wondering the entire time if her fiancé will find it first and come for me like he did the last time I crossed that line into his happy home.

two months ago

CHAPTER 2

While standing in the early morning line at the Panera Bread downtown, I heard a voice that brought my world to a standstill.

I couldn't help it, but I swung around and stared past the line of traders and suits behind me until my eyes located her. Hope McManus.

To me, she looked exactly like she had the last time I saw her three years, four months, and two days ago. (I was probably a little inaccurate with the months and days, but definitely right about it being three years). Except *this* sight of her was a happy one, as evidenced by that smile she displayed while speaking to another man, a guy in a suit who seemed to be our age—early thirties at the most and flirting with the notion of gray hair.

"You're up," the trader in the orange vest (not one of Landon's guys) told me, staring sternly past me at the girl behind the counter. I could read his impatience the same way he read market trends at the Merc all day.

I refocused, or tried pretty damn hard to at least reorient myself in reality, and stumbled through my regular order. Since hearing Hope's voice, I had lost both my focus and my appetite. I really didn't care if they used a regular egg instead of the egg whites I would have normally asked for, and keep the change. Yes, I know I gave you a twenty, just keep it, keep it, for real, I'm late, let's hurry up.

Get it together.

After paying for and collecting my food, I kept my head down and made my way toward the doors when she called me.

"Cameron!" It was an order, not a question. It was Hope.

I froze as she hurried over and planted herself right in front of me, taking my elbows so I couldn't run off and, well, die. That smile of hers killed me, those bright white teeth killed me, her hazel eyes killed me, her dark, wavy hair killed me. Everything about her was murderously perfect.

I smiled back at her (easy enough to do) and squeezed out in one long, run-on breath, "Hope, you look great what are you doing back in Chicago it's been so long since I've heard from you wow it's so nice to see you again are you living here or just visiting what have you been up to and how long will you be here?"

Hope laughed. Deep down, I figured she would do that—kill me some more with her essence before giving the knife a final turn in my chest for good measure.

I forced a laugh of my own; I didn't want to feel left out in our private chat in the middle of this busy Panera Bread. When I stopped acting like a donkey, she handed me a business card.

The first thing I noticed was that her last name hadn't changed. The second thing I noticed was the address. My face stiffened as I met her stare again. "That's the same building where I work," I said.

The smile melted off her lips. "I haven't seen you there. Are you new?"

I consulted the business card again. She was on the 14th floor at a company called Probst Financial Consultants LLC. I was on the 45th. Different elevators, but still a mystery that we hadn't crossed paths before.

I shrugged. "Been with SCF for three years this October. But anyway, we should—"

"Grab lunch," she finished for me, and that smile returned.

"Yes," I agreed, frowning like the professional banker I was supposed to be.

"And soon."

The man she had arrived with brought her coffee and nodded at me. His hands were full from carrying her order, as well as his own.

"Yes," I said with a nod that almost convinced me that I was back to normal. "Soon."

When we left Panera, Hope and her colleague steered left, and I turned right, even though we were all headed to the same building. I was sure my behavior would be interpreted as bizarre, but one surprise miracle in a single day was just about enough for me.

CHAPTER 3

That day, running into Hope at Panera sucked. A lot. Had I not already used the last of my annual sick day allowance this month—blame that one on a hard weekend of partying with Gordon and some of his poshy executive friends aboard a company jet to New York—I would've used it to get my head straight that day. Combine that with Newman on my ass about some of my past due, cross-selling reports, taking time off was definitely out of the question.

Speaking of Gordon, I called him after spending an hour Google-stalking Hope McManus, who didn't exist according to the fine folks in Mountain View, California. But she did exist; I had just seen her and stared into her eyes.

"Cam!" Gordon answered on the first ring.

Despite his extensive contact list of executives, Gordon was currently sentenced to a few years of stay-at-home dad, after leading a fast and hard life as an overpaid VP at Harris Financial Group. It wasn't so much the job that landed him that sentence; it was that after he *lost* his job four years post-financial crisis, he didn't tell Melinda.

It wasn't simply that she wasn't a fan of secrets between spouses—in hindsight, her anti-secrecy policy made sense. It was more that he had managed to burn through half of his seven-figure severance in a record-setting three weeks. And once his litigator wife clued in to his unemployment, she put a fast and firm end to the spending spree before their entire wealth evaporated on trips and cars and dinners and crazy trips to the islands. *Oops.*

So it made perfect sense to me why Gordon picked up midway through that first ring; he was supposed to be supervising his two young-ish kids before they headed off to private school. For Gordon, adult conversation had become something of a commodity.

"You won't believe it," I told him.

"Melinda's train derailed this morning?" he laughed and, as much as I knew he was joking, I also detected a bit of optimism in his tone.

"Worse. Hope works in my building."

Silence. It should not have surprised me to hear it.

"I, uh, I saw her this morning at Panera," I blurted out. "I don't normally eat that shit, but I had a craving. And we talked. She looks good, Gordo. I mean, she's wine."

"What the fuck are you talking about?" he asked, his tone radiating confusion. Again with the lack of adult-stimulation.

"Wine, Gordo. You know how it gets better with age?"

"That's cheese."

"Um, no," I said, but I was a little hesitant because my head was still clouded and spinning from running into Hope. "Gordo, cheese gets moldy with age."

There was a pause. "Shit," he said. "Hold on." There was some running and then, "Jeffrey, don't eat that!" Whining ensued, then Gordon said to his six-year-old, "You want an ice cream bar before we leave for school? Yeah? Then be quiet for ten minutes while I talk to Cam."

His parenting skills amazed me. Inspired me, in fact. Because if Jeffrey and Janelle—his nine-year-old daughter—hadn't died in the past three or so years during Gordon's daddy-daycare term, it was highly unlikely that I would inadvertently kill my own spawn. That is *if* I ever convinced Riley—or any other woman, namely Hope—to allow me to impregnate her.

"So you work with Hope?" he asked.

"No, she works for an accounting firm in the building. We're 'close,' but not that close."

"But you could see her again?"

"Yes," I said, letting out a long breath that somehow sounded hopeful and fearful at the same time.

"Don't." He said it without hesitation, in the same way a priest insists on the existence of God. "You should quit your job. Right-fucking-now before this gets out of hand. Spend the rest of your Harris severance in Mexico, drinking cheap beer and tequila, fucking Riley, and getting that tan back." He chuckled. "Fuck, I miss those three weeks."

CHAPTER 4

Gordon was right, and I knew it. After hanging up, I stepped away from my cubicle and started toward the stairs to the 46th floor, amazed by how many workspaces they could fit into such a relatively small space.

Higher-paid managers had cubes closer to the windows. Mine was the next row out. The admin staff occupied smaller cubes in the interior of the floor, where there was a fancy glass stairwell that hugged the walls of the elevator shaft and brought you upstairs to the upper-management and executive suites. Yes, that would be the building's 46th floor.

"Cam," I heard behind me, stopping me halfway up those beautiful stairs to our office's version of Heaven.

I turned and found Newman standing at the bottom stair, gripping the railing but otherwise motionless. His double chin spilled over the collar of his shirt, his gut threatening to pop a button. That was my boss, the physical and mental role model of health and sanity.

"What's up, Newman?"

His face turned red. My non-professional assessment blamed the angry color on high blood pressure, combined with early morning pepperettes, and his lack of exercise. He gave me a curt upward nod.

"Where are you going?"

I deliberately traced my stare along the stairwell, following the steps all the way up to the next level, then glared straight back at the man who wanted nothing more than to see me fall on my face and die. But judging by physical characteristics alone, he would be the first to do that. "I was going to the parking garage."

Newman wasn't one for humor. "Get back in your cube. I need that report."

I pointed upstairs. "Raj called."

Newman studied me, and I could tell that he was wondering whether it was within his professional scope to challenge me, to call my bluff.

So I reminded him, "The one person I wouldn't want to piss off, Newman? The guy that runs Human Resources."

He nodded, obviously seeing the logic in my argument and not quite in the mood to test his own employability at the moment. "When you're done, I'd like to see you in my office." He meant 'cube,' but guys like Newman preferred to never be corrected.

"Okay, I'll see you in your cube," I said, then continued my ascent to the executive floor, which was literally comparable to stepping out of the Bronx and into Beverly Hills.

"Hi, there, Cam," Chantal said. She was the receptionist up here, and she always smiled, always looked and smelled great. I bet she offered our biggest clients blowjobs; she was *that* good. "Here to see Raj?"

I nodded.

She sent him a private message, something we didn't have access to downstairs. By the time I sat down, Raj appeared, stepping through a pair of frosted-glass doors that looked innocent enough, but were actually bulletproof and electrified. After hours, anyway.

"Cam!" he said. Raj packed two hundred and twenty-five pounds onto his six-foot frame and was a lot like the Pakistani version of Charlie Hunnam. Or something like that. "Come into my office. Please."

I followed him past the security doors without touching them, always a little nervous each time I stepped into these hallways. His window office could easily fit eight cubicles. It had a big wooden desk, three client chairs, a six-person boardroom table, and a door. I sat in a client chair, and he settled behind the desk.

"What brings you upstairs, man?" he asked, linking his hands behind his head and reclining in his big leather chair. I waited for him to put his feet on his desk, then remembered that wasn't Raj's style; he would never put his dirty shoes on that desk because he preferred female employees on it instead. And, no, his wife did not work for our company.

I pointed at his computer monitor. "How many sick days do I have left, Raj?"

The smile started to melt away. "I believe you have access to that information through our EmployeeCentral intranet site and—"

I shook my head. "Raj, that wasn't the question."

The smile evaporated, and he sat straight in his chair. "You realize Mr. Newman has you on notice."

"Raj, we both know twenty sick days really isn't a whole lot."

He laughed at my comment. "Twenty is plenty! But you only have *fifteen*, Cameron, which is still five more than we had at Harris!"

I shook my head again. "Exactly. I need twenty. And if you can't swing that, then you need to give me one more. Just one more day, Raj."

I knew Raj hated finding himself in these situations because, just as another sick day could cost me my job, tampering with my personnel record could cost Raj his.

"Newman can't keep track of his own desk chair," I assured Raj. "And that's when he's sitting in it. So there's no chance he's been keeping top-quality tabs on my attendance since January. Trust me."

We proceeded to have a serious-as-a-tumor staring contest, which I won. My past employment at Harris Financial Services had allowed me to sit across the table from some of the most influential leaders in the financial services industry. Without a stone-cold stare, I would not have lasted as long as I had. Raj didn't have a snowball's chance in Miami of surviving my stare.

"You won't regret this, Raj," I promised, giving him a final nod of approval.

Like a loyal parent who can't say no to a petulant child, Raj sighed and faced his computer. I watched closely as he logged onto our personnel database, glancing over at me like he might have second thoughts about the crime he felt he was about to commit. I watched him navigate to the benefits page and reduce my sick-day count by one. The amount of times a pop-up window asked for appropriate-level authorization made me think we were changing the combination to the vault at the Federal Reserve.

Once he finished, he faced me, his dark face having turned a couple shades lighter. "I can't help you after this, man. Newman will come for you. Hard. He wants your balls."

I agreed with a nod; Newman's opinion of me was no secret to anyone with a pulse.

"What is this all about, Cam?"

I contemplated my response. Given Raj's VP role in our company, I didn't want to put him in a compromised position if he were ever interrogated about my plans for my next long weekend. Just as Raj had feigned calmness earlier, I sat back in my chair and laced my hands behind my head. Unlike Raj, I had no reservations about putting my dirty shoes on the desk that had seen a long laundry list of dirtier employees' asses.

"Raj, do you remember that time, six months ago? We were both working a little late, and your wife came by to bring you a warm dinner. You weren't expecting her, but I heard her calling for you, all the way from downstairs."

He shifted and loosened the tie around his neck, unbuttoning his collar like it had just gotten a little hot in here. No doubt, it had been steamy in here six months ago, while he and one of the administrators downstairs were risking their own marriages.

"Yes, I'm indebted to you, Cam. But how much longer do I need to cover for you?"

"Do you remember what you told me about Katja?" I gave

him my hard stare again.

The memory softened him a little; that frown turned upside down, as if he was remembering the exact position she had assumed on his desk that night, her legs spread and ankles held wide apart. He actually had to shake his head to find his way back to reality.

"You told me you were in love with a Russian—"

"Belarusian," he corrected.

"Whatever, Raj. The point is that you risked your marriage for a woman who would never be with you."

"We still see each other on occasion," he admitted, maybe a little defensively. And then the puzzle pieces dropped into place, and he saw the full picture. "Oh shit, Cam. This is about a woman?" He didn't need my answer. "I am happy to hear that. Why do you need time off, though; are you taking her somewhere?"

"Nowhere," I admitted, but it was a lie because three years ago, she had given me an itinerary of sorts. I had just been too stupid to recognize it until now. "I just need to hear four words from her. And I need a sick day to make that happen."

CHAPTER 5

The following day, I changed my lunch hour and paper-bagged my meal so I could eat in the building's vast lobby. From an interior bench at the windows that overlooked the courtyard, I watched people come and go, never taking my eyes off the even-numbered elevators. An hour passed, and I never saw Hope McManus step on or off the elevators, though.

Instead, I heard her voice beside me. "Come here often?"

It startled me. I jumped off the bench, and she laughed. It was in her face, those hazel eyes that reminded me of a part of myself I had long forgotten.

Once my heartbeat calmed down, I gave her my biggest and brightest smile. Fuck, she truly was perfection all rolled up in the shape and form of a human being, wrapped in an innocent and professional skirt and purple button-down shirt that my memory told me smelled like a cocktail of Tide, sweet perfume, and something uniquely Hope.

"A little jumpy, Cameron?" She stepped closer to me, bringing her lips so close to my ear that the left side of my body went numb. "You're stalking me, aren't you?"

I didn't have an answer for her.

"You have my number," she reminded me, stepping back.

"Why couldn't you call like a big person? I could've brought my lunch, and we could've had a picnic, right here in the lobby of this building that our companies share."

"What are you doing here?" I asked, my face and tone friendly despite the broken spirit behind those words. "Why haven't I heard from you? I mean, three years ago…"

She kept smiling, but I could see that mentioning what had happened three years ago bothered her. A lot. Placing her left hand on my chest, she told me to relax. "I'm not crazy like that anymore."

"I wasn't exactly thinking of the crazy part," I said, still playing friendly. "And it wasn't crazy, by the way. It's just that it would've been nice knowing you're here."

"Maybe we should have dinner."

The sunlight caught on her oversized ring—a wedding band? What the *fuck* was this, *Kick Cam in the nuts* day? But all I did was nod. "Tonight?"

She shrugged. "A little short on notice, but sure. That sounds good. Do you want to meet at my office on the fourteenth floor after work? We can go straight from here?"

I told her I lived a few blocks away, we could go to my place and—

Shaking her head, that smile got bigger. "Don't think so, Cameron. Let's just meet at my office, and we'll catch a cab."

I nodded. Before I realized it, I was walking with her toward the elevators. "Where are we going?"

"Signature Room. It's in the story I sent you three years

ago."

It should not have surprised me that she would want to go there.

"What's that look for?" she asked, and I realized I had rolled my eyes.

"Tourist trap."

"Maybe, but I've never been…" Her elevator arrived, and she stepped aboard, swinging around and flashing me one final smile so I could glance at her pure white teeth as those doors started closing.

"Then that's where we'll go! I'll make the reservations!" But they were closed, and the elevator was already making its ascent, and I realized I had left the other half of my sandwich on the bench.

I wasn't hungry anymore, so I didn't bother heading back to get it.

CHAPTER 6

Since I lived downtown, I left work early. Newman was in meetings all afternoon and wouldn't miss me. I needed a quick shower and to change into a fresh shirt and jacket, but in my big rush back to the building, I got held up—the el train was super slow, and the crowds were so heavy they delayed me.

It was interesting and irritating, hurrying against the current of pedestrians eager to get home, while I was impatient to get back to work. I was a little late reaching the office building. When I entered the lobby, I found it completely vacant, and the air conditioning felt refreshing against my perspiring forehead. I could've heard a pin drop in there, and I wondered if maybe I had missed her, if she had gone home after I failed to show up like we agreed.

But then I heard the *ding* of the elevators, followed by the *click-clack* of a woman's heels on the marble floor.

And there she was.

My heart stopped, and I held my breath as she came around the corner, still beautiful in that professional skirt suit from earlier today. When she saw me, her face didn't give any indication of happiness or annoyance. Which was frustrating because I had previously been something of an expert at arousing both of those emotions in her.

"You were supposed to meet me upstairs," she said.

I hadn't noticed it earlier, but I definitely noticed it now. Although she seemed like the same woman from three years ago, she wasn't. She had changed a little, aged. There were lines at the corners of her eyes and around the edges of her mouth. But her eyebrows were absolutely stunning, and she was more beautiful than ever. Not like cheese, but wine, the finest kind.

"I know," I answered at last. "I'm sorry."

Her face crunched up, and she shot me a sideways stare. "Did you go home and change?"

I brushed my hand down the front of my jacket, a newer one that fit me a little better than the one I had been wearing this morning. "I should probably go grab a cab."

Hope's half-grin told me she knew exactly what I was doing by avoiding her question. "No," she said. "Let's walk."

"In those heels?" I asked as she started toward the lobby doors.

She shrugged. "You'll carry me if I can't walk back, won't you, Cameron?" That part of her hadn't changed, the part that wanted to be in my arms. And that was how I knew that *all* of me hadn't changed either, because the mere thought of having her in my arms again sucked the air out of my lungs and made my stomach jump at the thought, the *hope* that she wouldn't be able to walk back.

CHAPTER 7

Our window table at the Signature Room was ideal. Because we arrived so early, the restaurant was not very busy, and we didn't have to wait long to be seated. I watched Hope's round, wide eyes as she admired the city and lake views.

During our walk here, she admitted to never even entering the John Hancock, despite living in Chicago for nearly two years already. "Although," she said, "it probably would've been closer to three if we had been able to sell the house."

"So does this fiancé of yours have a name?" I asked, then put the glass of water to my lips to avoid admitting something stupid like how I hated him already.

"Yes, it's still Matt." If my question bothered her, she didn't let on. It bothered me, so I kept drinking the water while she kept staring out those windows. "And before you ask, I'll remind you that he's something of an accounting god. It's why we moved here in the first place and why we're moving to San Francisco in a couple of months…" At this point, she steered her eyes to mine while I held the now-empty glass to my lips. "… so, yes, he's got lots of money."

At least now I knew why she cared to tell me that last little bit of information about Matt the Motherfucker, the geriatric dickhead.

If getting dumped by a spouse for a "younger model" burned women, then losing the love of your life to a wealthier lover burned men. Hope knew this, but I didn't let on that it bothered me. I placed the glass of water back on the table. It bothered me a lot.

"What about you, Cameron? Last I heard you ended up getting married after all. What's her name again? And what did you tell her about going out to dinner with me tonight after what happened three years ago?"

I started to tell her about Riley, her flowing blonde hair and blue eyes, her energetic *youth*, but before I could get into the parts that would sting her as much as her "he's got lots of money" bullshit stung me, Hope cut me off.

"Completely unnecessary, Cameron," she said, rolling her eyes like she had already read the headlines.

I allowed a numb nod. All of this "let's be friends and talk about our respective partners" bullshit felt somewhat foreign to me, like that moment of disorientation before the migraine set in.

Hope sipped from her water. "You never forget the name of the woman who shatters your dreams. No need to elaborate or remind me."

I started praying for the waitress to come and take our order, but because I knew quite well that my prayers were not the type to get anyone's attention, I asked the one question that had been on my mind all afternoon. "Tell me about that book from three years ago."

That question had an effect on her. For the first time since seeing her at Panera, Hope stumbled off that high and mighty tightrope she had been walking. Her eyes shifted to her hands, and she kept them there, safely away from me.

"You want to talk about it?" I asked, knowing quite well that I needed to stay on top here. I needed to bring her back to my level, which was right here on Earth. Technically speaking, it was right here, ninety-five floors above street level.

CHAPTER 8

After dinner, we walked north to the beach. Crossing Lake Shore was a pain in the ass. We could've taken the tunnel, but decided to risk our lives instead. I raced across the street, watching and laughing as Hope struggled in her heels. By the time we reached the walking path, she removed those death-trap Gucci shoes and carried them. I figured she did that so she wouldn't be tempted to hold my hand.

We had enjoyed a nice dinner at the Signature Room, and this calm walk felt perfect, both of us with big grins on our faces, the sun still going strong, and the rush of commuters behind us. We stayed in the slow lane, allowing cyclists and rollerbladers to speed past, none of them bugging us. I imagined Heaven would feel exactly like this moment.

"It's great that you're in Chicago," I said at last, and the silence that ensued told me I probably should not have crossed that line. So I crossed another one. "I missed you."

We walked without speaking, and then she told me a little more about this novel someone named Emma Payne had shared with her. "What you don't know is that these two people were strangers. They met on an airplane and have this instant connection. They're both married, and Olivia is in Chicago for a short period of time. But for him, for Oliver, he goes home. He lives in Winnetka, just like Matt and I do in our big mini-mansion with a four-car garage. But when Oliver gets there, he finds that his wife has taken their two kids to Wisconsin, to her parents' summer house for the weekend."

"Four-car garage, huh?

"I knew you'd like that."

I gave her a knowing nod. "I think I know where this is headed."

"Trust me, you don't."

"Sure, I do. Obviously, this Oliver dude fucks Olivia all weekend long, and then his wife returns early to catch them."

Hope shook her head, rolling her eyes. "It was their anniversary weekend. So Oliver is disappointed and, instead of spending the weekend alone, he meets up with Olivia—their names are so close that it's really confusing to read at times, but Emma insists on those specific names—and he takes her out to dinner. At the Signature Room."

"Figures..."

"Like us, they have a great time. I imagine it being exactly like our night has been so far. The laughing and flirting and all of that." She tucked her hair behind her ear, allowing her hand to hover over lips for a moment—covering up a smirk, perhaps—and then she refocused on me again.

"Flirting?" I asked, and then brushed my hand against hers before giving it a gentle squeeze.

With the snappy reflexes of a feline, Hope swung her shoe at my face. "Cameron! You're pushing it!"

Luckily, I avoided her attempted assault with grace and humility and a crazy laughter that sucked all the air out of my lungs. Once I calmed down, I told her to continue. "So after dinner, what happens next for Oliver and Olivia? Is that when they fuck?"

"Actually, they don't 'fuck,' Cameron. They go for a walk." She frowned.

A walk? Like this one?

"You know, I don't believe you didn't read it…"

"So their time was a lot like this," I said, dismissing her statement about not believing me because she was right; after all of these years she was still fucking right. I waved elaborately at the path before us. "And then they fuck at the beach? Is that how it happens for us, too?"

I stepped back, afraid she might take another swing at me. But she didn't.

"I won't hurt you," she said with a taste of evil to her tone. "Which is something you said to me once. Except unlike you, I'll stick to my promise."

"Ouch." I pressed a hand to my chest. "*Touché.* But you're wrong, you've hurt me plenty."

She ignored my comment and continued with the story, with *Our Story*. I loved hearing her version of it because these were details I hadn't spent too much time memorizing. "They walk Michigan Ave under the lights. And end up at her hotel."

"*Bow-chica-wow-wow.*"

"No," she sighed, and I could tell she worked hard at suppressing her irritation with my childishness. "All they do is lie in bed. They talk all night, they laugh and smile and memorize every little detail about each other—their cheekbones, the lines around their eyes and lips, the mole on her neck, the scar underneath his chin, all of that sappy shit that people like to read about."

"Like we used to do," I said, remembering our last night together in that hotel room, lying awake and fighting sleep, tracing her face with the back of my fingers before… "Do they kiss at least?"

Hope shook her head, her attention elsewhere like I might have lost her to the fantasy of what three years ago could have been for us. "No, there's not even an attempt. Because what these two people have is special, Cameron. It's not physical. Although, they both have these really hot and steamy thoughts about going where they don't go. And it's not about that one night. In fact, with them it's not about any given night. It's about…"

I faked a yawn as we reached the beach. I jumped into the sand, knowing right away that I would regret it. I hated the gritty sand in my shoes. "Bullshit. It's always about the physical, Hope."

"I disagree," she argued, her subtle frown suggesting that maybe she didn't quite believe me. "And it's definitely not about that for Oliver and Olivia. For them, it's about…I don't know, it's about the *moment.* That's all that matters to them because it's all they'll ever have. A moment." Her voice hitched a notch and, when I glanced over at her, I scrutinized her face, searching for a hint as to where that fault line might lay.

In my head, I replayed Hope's words, each one of them because I had memorized them. As was the case with Oliver and Olivia, all that mattered to me was *this* moment.

I wanted to believe that *our* love—this thing between Hope and I—was as strong as Oliver and Olivia's, but I didn't truly know that. I knew how *I* felt. But Hope? I figured she had given up on us long ago, walking away without so much as a glance back. It had been cold, but she was stronger than that, way better than to cling to an unlikely fairytale. Still, some part of me wanted to believe that the hint of emotion in her voice had come from that abandoned love, from that belief that we were exactly like the Oliver and Olivia that she had written about.

"It's a touching story," she admitted, heaving a deep, cleansing breath. "I've read it hundreds of times."

I kept my mouth shut as she settled onto the sand next to me. We watched the water, the soft waves lapping against the sand where a couple of young kids were building mounds of goop that looked like something the cows back home could produce.

Hope sighed. "You ever wonder why we ran into each other, Cameron? I mean, two months before I'm scheduled to pack up and move across the country again. It's weird. Kind of like how I ran into you three years ago. Right before your wedding."

"Why aren't *you* married?" I asked, instead of talking about myself. I had wondered that question a million times since we ran into one another the last time.

She shrugged. "It's not what Matt and I want."

I chuckled, still watching those young kids playing together. They were clearly brother (older) and sister (younger). Their mother was reading a book with a white cover and some strange symbol on the front. While the boy added to his pile of fake cow shit, the sister filled a pail of water and threw it at the boy—the entire pail, not just the water, so it was a good thing she missed him—and then she ran off, laughing while the boy whined and complained. The entire scene made me smile.

"You know that Matt's older than I am," she elaborated, sitting on her shins and shifting to stay comfortable. I wondered if she would allow me to pick the sand out of her knees. "And with our careers, we're just not in a position where we can lay down any roots, so marriage really isn't a priority for us."

"Sounds like you're trying to convince yourself more than you're trying to convince me, Hope." Although I found myself far more interested in seeing how this argument between the brother and sister would unravel, I *felt* Hope's glare burning into the side of my head. She knew I was right, didn't she?

"What the fuck is that supposed to mean, goob?"

I nodded at the kids. "How much do you want to bet that little girl kicks her big brother's ass?" At that point, the boy tackled her, and the mother was hurrying over to separate them. "Maybe not here at the beach. But tonight at home, right before bed when they're both overly tired, she'll sneak up on him and give him a cheap shot."

"I don't need to be married," Hope continued with a

defensive tone that suggested she was on trial. "Why would you say that, Cameron? You're being an asshole."

I allowed my eyes to meet hers as the argument between the brother and sister fizzled and the mediation process failed to hold my attention. "Maybe you're right and there's a reason we met two months before your big move—"

"So you can preach your idea of marriage to me?"

"Maybe." I stared up at the sky. "Or maybe it was just so I could remind you of who you are. You know, the real Hope. The one who lives deep, deep down behind that hard candy shell."

"Is that what happened three years ago?" she asked. "I reminded you of who you are?"

"Maybe."

Hope's face tightened. For the span of a heartbeat, I thought she might take another swing at me. Instead, she stood up and started walking away. "Epic fail, Cameron," she called back, swinging her shoes in her hands, the back of her skirt crumpled to show a little more thigh than I had seen back at the office building. "All you've done is remind me of what an asshole you are."

I stood up and chased after her, closing the gap of a half-dozen feet that she had spread between us as the sand squeezed into my shoes and socks somehow. "Hey," I said, keeping my voice soft and empathetic. "I didn't mean to piss you off." I didn't dare reach out to touch her, to slow her down. I knew to keep my hands to myself and not distract her from her little march. "Maybe I don't know you anymore. But when I did? When I knew you like nobody else did?

Hope, listen to me."

She kept walking. But I never expected *easy* from Hope. Ever.

"You talk about moments between Oliver and Olivia in that story?" I asked, although it was more of a statement, and I had to pick up the pace to keep up with her. "Well, those days when you opened yourself up to me, they were the most beautiful moments of my life." I swallowed hard. That anger in her face made for one hell of a barrier to this deep-down honesty spewing from my lips. "Sorry. Maybe I was confusing the memory of those moments with who I *thought* you were." I glanced over at her and saw that she had softened a bit, her perfect eyebrows more relaxed than two sentences ago.

We walked in silence for what felt like an eternity, my words hanging over us like molasses clouds.

"Hope, what are we doing here?" I wanted to grab her by the shoulders and shake the answers out of her, get to that emotional paradise she had walked out on three years ago, the place I had fought so hard for.

Silence, as she kept walking. To my eyes and senses, she seemed to consider letting me in, allowing me back on the other side of those gates she had shut and locked.

"I'm sorry, Cameron. I need to get home."

PRESENT DAY

CHAPTER 9

7:38 AM

Midway through my second lap in some scene out of Gran Turismo 6 for the Xbox One, my phone vibrates. I don't have time to pause the race with its better-than-reality graphics, so I quickly snap up the phone and stare at the jAppe chat.

My heart pounds underneath my chest at the response on the screen.

Hope: Sorry. I can't. Too much to get done before the big move next week.

Fuck.

And then:

Hope: I'm really sorry :-(

Double-fuck. I type a quick response.

Me: I'll meet you at the Ogilvie.

Less than three seconds pass before I have her rebuttal.

Hope: Don't make me embarrass you, Cameron!

Done.

I check the time and determine that 1) she has already boarded the 316 Metra train to Chicago and 2) I don't have much time left to firm up the details of our day—possibly our *last* day—together before she moves away.

The next thing I do is dial Gordon's number. Of course he picks up before the first ring has ended; those kids are killing him.

"You need a job," I tell him, watching the time because I have less than half an hour to get to the train station.

"Funny you should—"

"I need your Tesla, Gordo," I interrupt, stepping out the of Bat Cave and walking to the front closet. I slide the doors open and stare at my small wardrobe of jackets, shoes, and other fine apparel on one half. The other side is vacant.

"What? No fucking way!"

"I'll pay your electricity bill for a fucking month. I just need the car."

"What's wrong with your BMW?" he asks, his voice pitched high like it always does when he gets anxious.

"It's not a Bentley." I file through a couple of jackets and remember the weather forecast for this afternoon—89F. Screw the jacket. I squat to get a closer look at the shoes. Hope will notice the shoes, and the nicer they are, the more relaxed she'll be. Which means she'll be more inclined to play sick day with me.

"This isn't a good idea," Gordon tells me. "I know what you're up to, and it's a fucking horrible idea, Cam."

"I know." I grab a pair of Skechers. Not the Chucks, not the Mephistos, or the Hush Puppies, but the brown Skechers. They're clean and unpretentious. They look good with these jeans, the Tommy's that make my legs look both lean and solid. "But I'm doing it anyway, Gordo, and I need your car."

Time check—7:43.

"Can you meet me at the Art Institute at noon?" I ask him.

The huffing and puffing on the other end of the line is an embarrassment. For Gordon. "I can't give you my car!"

"Is the battery dead? Because if it's not, I really don't understand your hesitation. It's a car, not your firstborn."

"Not only will Miranda castrate me if she finds out I'm lending it to *you*, of all fucking people, but this is just bad news!"

"Art Institute. Noon. Or you're flying on your own the next time you have a crazy boy weekend with Josh and Landon."

I hear some groaning, then Gordon tells Jeffrey it's not pancake Tuesday, not even close, so eat the damn Rice Krispies, because he's on the phone. To me, he offers a heavy sigh and asks, "What's in it for me?"

"I just told you," I say, keeping my patience in check. "My companionship on the next boys' trip."

"Okay, right, yes you said that." Gordon in panic mode is a

time-waster even when he's coming down off that hyperactive high. "Then tell me what you're after with Hope. What's the point of this? I dealt with your bullshit the last time. Remember three years ago? I don't want Riley hurt again, and I can't be your accomplice in this."

I pause at the front door, checking my pockets and making sure I have the keys. My hands feel clammy all of a sudden, and my stomach growls. "I need her to say four words. That's it. That's the point."

"Four words?" He chuckles. "Which ones?"

"'I'm leaving you.'"

"I think that's three words," he corrects me, and all traces of chuckling are dead.

"Only if you think the contraction of 'I' and 'am' reduces it to three, Gordon. So technically, it's still four words." I give him a fraction of a heartbeat to say something else. When he doesn't, I remind him to meet me at the Art Institute at noon. "With the Tesla."

"Hey, Cam?" he adds, but the tone teeters on begging. "Tell me you're not going to fuck her once she tells you that she's leaving you."

"Oh, those four words aren't for me. They're for Matt."

I hang up before he can realize just how serious I am. Time check—7:47.

I'm left with twenty-eight minutes to reach the Ogilvie Transportation Center, so I have to sprint the one and a half miles. Just to be safe.

two months ago

CHAPTER 10

The 363 train left downtown Chicago at 7:35 PM. I had attempted to convince Hope to stay out a little longer and grab some drinks or even come see the condo I purchased at a steep discount in 2012, using a good chunk of the Harris severance that I invested and increased seven-fold in less than a few months. But she had insisted on going home.

"Alone," she added as I joined her on the train.

"No way." She knew—of course she knew—that I would never let her off that easily.

She rolled her eyes and slid into a forward facing bench, crossing her arms and staring out the green-tinted window. Within minutes, the train started moving, so the awkwardness didn't last long.

"Do you miss Miami?" I asked as the train emerged from the station and sailed along the tracks into the casual early-evening daylight.

"Isn't Riley, your *wife*, going to wonder where you are? You haven't checked your Blackberry the entire time we've been out."

"Neither have you." I shifted a little closer to her despite the snootiness in her last comment, but she shook her head at me and returned to staring out the window like that might make me disappear. I played it safe, kept the tone soft and playful. "What is it, Hope?"

"I don't know where you think this is headed," she told the

window, "but it's not going there."

"We can't be friends?"

"You're clearly incapable of friendship, Cameron."

"How so?" It had been intended as a joke, but her response insulted me a little. Now I was curious.

"And I don't trust you. I don't trust any married man who jumps on a train with me in an attempt to ruin my happy home."

I let up a bit with my persistence, just in case her mention of a "happy home" had an iota of truth to it. "Riley's not home tonight. So she doesn't care if I'm on a train heading into Winnetka or scuba diving with Gordon in the Turks and Caicos like we did last spring. It's nice there, have you ever been? You'd look really good on those beaches, the sand on your thighs…"

She smiled at my inability to stay focused on a single topic at a time. "Matt won't be happy if he comes home and finds you in the house."

I shrugged. "I don't need to see your bedroom, so I'm fine with sticking to the kitchen like a regular guest. Remember what happened in your kitchen in Miami—"

"Matt still hates you after what happened." She pulled her attention away from the window so she could look at me.

I allowed an understanding nod. "I can't really blame him."

Hope showed me her serious eyes. "So you're not walking home with me."

"We'll see," I said, showing her my serious eyes, too.

CHAPTER 11

At the Winnetka station, we disembarked together, but I stayed on the platform and watched Hope walk away while the train bell clamored off the retaining walls, and the big beast rumbled onward. Once she reached the stairs leading up to street level, Hope stepped aside to let the other late commuters pass, and then turned to me as I stood alone, purposely hunching my shoulders and kicking at invisible pebbles like a lost child.

"Goob!" she called out. And then, when I didn't respond, "Cameron!"

I raised my attention to her. When she waved me over, I launched into an elaborate and dramatic sprint, something straight out of *Forrest Gump*, projecting my arms out to the side like airplane wings as I got closer to her, then scooping her up off the ground and twirling her around. She didn't fight me or try to wiggle out of my deathly squeeze. In fact, I even heard a giggle escape before she forced a fake disgusted grunt.

"Let. Me. Go."

"Never," I announced, but ended up releasing her anyway. It was getting a little awkward. Even at her featherweight one hundred and twenty pounds, she started to feel a little heavy to my lazy arms after a couple of twirls. "Change your mind about fucking me in the kitchen?"

"Hardy har har," she said, glaring at me. "Like I said, you're incapable of this friendship thing."

"Who says that anymore?" I asked, ignoring her friendship statement. "Even my dead grandmother doesn't say 'hardy har har.'"

We reached street level, and she pointed past the main intersection. "There's still a Barney's across the street. We can have coffee like two friends while we wait for the next train, which is in half an hour."

"It'll start getting dark by then," I said, forcing a frown and shaking my head. "I can't let you walk home by yourself in the dark."

Shaking her head, she assured me she would be fine. "I live less than two blocks away; I've done it alone before. A lot." A pause. "You still like Barney's?"

"Only every day when I'm not running into my soul mate at Panera."

She punched me in the shoulder. "Cameron! Stop that, or I won't stick around! And then you'll have to wait alone for the train."

For being so close to Chicago, Winnetka felt like its own little village in the middle of some laid-back corner of the country. Despite the time of day, there were couples walking the cozy and somewhat trendy downtown streets. At Barney's—my favorite boutique espresso bar since Hope had introduced me to the place three years ago—there were couples sitting out front at the bistro tables. It surprised me just how popular this high-caffeine joint could be at this time of night.

Inside, I ordered a biscotti and my usual non-fat double-shot cappuccino. I didn't hear what Hope ordered; I just paid for it. We sat inside at a table in the back corner, where people wouldn't waste time bothering us. I imagined this being the same table where Olivia had waited for Oliver, then remembered she had taken a table on the back patio.

"Why not out back?" I wondered.

"This is a compromise, right here," she explained, poking at the table. "You need to smile more often, Cameron."

"Remember three years ago?" I asked, testing the waters again. "I think I smiled a lot back then."

She stirred her drink—either a latté like she used to prefer, or a cappuccino (they looked the same to me in these take-out cups)—even though she hadn't added anything to it that would require stirring. "No, let's not do this," she said with a bit of a sigh.

"That Friday night when you showed up," I started, glancing up at her to see how she would respond. When she simply stared back, I continued. "I wasn't expecting you. Not that Friday night or any other night come to think of it. I thought it was over between us. That I was forgotten."

Her attention lowered to her drink again. Her cheeks looked heavy to me, confirming my assumption that this was the last thing she wanted to talk about tonight.

"I never stopped thinking about you," I promised. I sipped my hot drink, hoping the liquid would burn some common sense back into me. But it didn't—it hurt my mouth, but that was about all it achieved. "Every day since and every day before that visit, I thought about you."

When Hope returned her attention, her eyebrows tightened, and she shook her head at me. I imagined this was the same look she gave her accounting clients when they had some serious tax issues that even David Copperfield couldn't fix or make disappear.

I tried to mirror her serious-as-fuck expression. "I don't have to go back to your place, Hope. I can walk to the train station all by myself. In fact, I don't have to see you ever again…but the reality remains that I'll never stop thinking about you. About us."

"You broke me," she answered quickly, and the words crushed me. "You seem to forget that, Cameron. We had a promise. A *promise.*" Her voice cracked a little, reminding me of earlier when we were talking about *Our Story* at the beach. This time, she didn't get up and walk away. She simply took a deep breath to regain her strength. It worked. Now there was strength, hard and merciless, tightening every muscle in her face. "I came for you. I called, I wrote, I tried everything. Do you know what I thought? All those years, I thought I did something. I thought I—"

"And then, when you had me, you pushed me away," I said, my voice a little louder than I had intended. A few of the people seated around us cast curious glances our way. I remembered Gordon's eyes on me, the heat of rejection on my skin after a night of loving her, all of her and *just her.* I leaned forward on the small table and whispered, "I gave all of myself to you, Hope. You did nothing wrong, it was all so right, but then I watched you walk away without looking back. What was I supposed to do?"

"I wanted you to *fight* for me," she said, her scowl stern enough that there was no misunderstanding as to which one of us dominated this conversation. "You said you'd fight for the rest of your life, that you'd always fight for me. For our love." The bulging vein on her neck suggested anger. "But you didn't."

I felt the temperature rising on my cheeks, suddenly wishing I hadn't agreed to this "friendly" coffee thing. "I gave you *exactly* what you asked for. You're welcome for that, by the way. You're welcome for the sacrifices I made, every last one while you lived that perfect life that you *chose* for yourself."

She shook her head at me, as if she were disgusted with what I had just said. The reality was that she probably recognized just how wrong she was here. Miami was not all that long ago. I doubted that she had forgotten it already.

We sipped on our respective drinks, letting our tempers cool. I could hear a ringing in my ears—a sound only Hope could trigger in me—and I recognized that the chatter around us had died down considerably.

I was the first to speak, leaning even closer to her while whispering the words, "I loved you more than I have ever loved anything or anyone else in my life, Hope. It's irreplaceable."

"Then why was I crushed more? Because when I found you playing house with Riley…" She couldn't finish, and looked away instead.

"We were a *month* from getting married," I reminded her with a hiss.

"But you made a promise to *me*."

I sat back, ready to give up.

Although she wasn't crying, she wiped at her eyes. She still looked good for spending so much time in that suit, and I didn't want to be the one to break that image of perfection. "Forget it, Cameron. This never gets us anywhere."

"No," I said. I didn't care if the people across the street could hear me. "It always brings us right back to this. To this moment where you keep pushing me away."

"I'm as good as married," she said, faking a laugh. "You *are* married." She threw her hands up. "You're too late. I pushed you away, you walked away, and then we had these years, these wasted years between us. And now you're just too fucking late because after Labor Day, I'm moving to San Francisco. Happy?"

I finished my capp in one final sip, then stood. I felt her stare on me, but I refused to look at her. There were a few other guys at Barney's, watching me to see what I would do. Did they think this was a domestic issue? I wondered and chuckled in my head. But they minded their own business.

I stepped away from the table without saying goodbye to the woman I have loved from the moment I met her, nearly twenty years ago at a neighborhood park.

I walked out to the street, oblivious to everything around me. I knew my way to the train station. Even though I was excessively early, I figured the time alone could help me calm down and figure out how such a great night had gone south so quickly. How had I gone from memorizing each word to wishing I hadn't seen her at Panera Bread?

Then I heard, "Cameron!"

It was just like yesterday, except this time her voice wore a layer of heartache.

I kept walking. Obviously in my moment of childishness, I didn't realize that Hope knew how to walk, too. Or run. Because that was what she did—she ran to catch up to me, her heels betraying any attempt at sneaking up on me that she may have entertained.

"Cameron," she repeated, her voice firm. "You never listen to me. Never."

"I've listened to your silence for all of these years, Hope. Look what listening has done for me." I stopped at the intersection because the signal said so. "All you do is keep pushing me away. What's wrong with me? Why can't I just let go of you?"

I turned to face her just as a silver Bentley GT rolled to a stop beside us.

"Shit," she whispered, and, despite her dry eyes, I saw enough emotion in them to know that she suffered from the same tear in her heart as I did. Our conversation had ended, I saw that, too. "That's Matt."

I smiled and waved at the tinted driver's side window, swallowing that lump of disappointment and burying it deep down like I had for all of these years.

It rolled open. Matt looked pissed. "What's going on here?" he asked.

"Relax, Matt," I said, amazed at how someone like Hope could run her fingers through that kind of salt and paper coif, no matter how clean cut he might be. "We were on the same train tonight, it's all good."

He didn't like my bullshit excuse and signaled Hope to the passenger side. She walked away without a word, without even looking back. *Déjà vu, anyone?*

"You should know something, Matt," I said as she climbed into that expensive car, my insides burning and wishing I could step on his douchebag excuse for a face.

"What's that, dickhead?"

"You might want to change the sheets when you get home."

I was prepared for him to jump out of the car and chase me, but he was old—probably his mid-forties was my guess—and I figured I'd tire that old geriatric fuck out long before he could ever reach me. Instead, he rolled the window up and drove off at a casual speed. Not even a "fuck you" or middle finger salute; he just drove off.

"That sucked," I said, then realized I had missed my opportunity to cross the street.

Karma.

CHAPTER 12

Back at the condo, I kicked my shoes into the closet, aware of the classical music and the savory odors of dinner. I headed straight to the Bat Cave, passing Riley at the dining table, noticing she had set a place for me—a tasty chicken entrée, a salad, and a glass of wine. That bullshit lie I had given Hope about Riley being away was just that—bullshit. If she had known Riley was waiting for me, she never would have agreed to our date in the first place.

"It's the Ontario cab you like," Riley said, her voice soft and unassuming. Her long fingers with their dark polish raised the wine glass to her red lips, and she looked beautiful doing it.

"I'm not hungry."

Inside the Bat Cave, I closed the sliding French doors and kept the lights off, dropping into Topsy. It got dark in here, despite the glass panes in the doors. It was a deafening darkness that truly allowed you to escape the world of real life. I watched the door, though, waiting for Riley's shadow to appear because I knew she would worry. I rarely bypassed dinner—and never the Reif Estates cabernet—unless I was having one of those days. When her shadow finally appeared, it hovered there for a beat before she knocked.

I didn't respond, so she asked if I was okay.

"Just need a bit of time," I answered, working hard to keep the expression of self-pity out of my voice.

This wasn't fair to Riley. She knew. Three years ago, she had allowed me to bury this bullshit under a heap of denial. She knew, and it wasn't fair to do this to her.

She knew it now, too. It would kill her. Three years ago, it nearly killed her. But this time it was killing her more. These past three years of trying, of reaching for something that would forever remain just beyond her fingertips, and tonight it had slipped even further away.

"Are you going to eat your dinner?" she asked.

I remained silent. After a bit of time, her shadow dimmed, the classical music disappeared, and all I had left was the darkness and blinding silence.

Time to deal with some demons.

CHAPTER 13

Even though I could've used that sick day that Raj had arranged to clear my head, I didn't call in sick at work the next day. I also didn't shave or iron my shirt. I walked with the downtown crowd to the office building and, as much as I would love to say I didn't even bother looking for Hope among the lobby herd, the only happiness I enjoyed that morning was the very prospect of seeing her.

I had scripted exactly what I would say to her, how I would apologize for unsuccessfully confronting Matt, and beg for another evening, another chance before she moved away for good. But I didn't see her, so the mental script was unnecessary. I felt like I had lost her again, that these next two months would turn into the same dust as the rest of my time without her.

Before boarding the elevator, I retrieved my phone, scrolled through my contacts to Newman's line, but I hung up before pressing CALL. I had a plan. I needed to stick to it. Today wasn't the day. I pocketed the phone and boarded the next elevator.

On the 45th floor, I walked straight to my cube, sat down, and fired up the computer. As was his routine, Newman made the rounds at a quarter to nine. When he stopped at my cube, he asked me who had fucking died. Nice guy, but then again I never would mistake him for a grief counselor.

"Rough night, that's all," I answered, lacing my hands behind my head and showing off my incredibly wrinkled shirt because I knew it would drive him nuts, almost as much as it would grate on my OCD. "How are the boys upstairs? Keeping you busy, Newman?"

He grunted, his face turning red as he hitched up his pants. "How many sick days do you have left, huh, Cam?" He knew the answer. He was just being the same fucktart he normally was. And it was only worse now because he sensed my weakness. "Would've been nice to call in 'tired' and get caught up on some sleep, huh, Cam?"

"I'll have those single-purchase buying trends to you by noon," I said, ignoring his remarks. But he had already wandered off to wish someone else a venomously good morning.

I turned back to my computer and tried to lose myself in my profession, which involved analyzing client purchasing behaviors in order to customize their relationship with Second City Financial. For instance, if a client uses one of our company-branded American Express cards at a florist's, followed or preceded by a charge at a tuxedo rental shop, and then booking a limo, we could deduce that there is a wedding in this client's future.

We could then align this client with some of our affiliates to tailor recommendations, advice, and other relevant solutions specifically catered to their life stage. For the newlywed in this illustration, we could align him or her with a real-estate broker who happened to be one of our more profitable clients, who would sell them a house and ensure that the client finances their purchase through our mortgage unit. Through that mortgage, we could also offer high-margin insurance products and tremendously increase the profitability of a client that was previously just an American Express user.

Although this was similar to my role at Harris, I had been far more highly regarded there. But after multiplying my severance on derivatives and using the winnings to purchase the condo, I had been desperate, and Raj had insisted on creating this position here at SCF. While it kept me busy and allowed for a regular paycheck, it also meant accepting that I had become a little less than a peon. They had me reporting to Newman, the Nazi manager who suffered from textbook SMS (Short-Man Syndrome). Newman ran our product management group. He was a dickhead and saw no value in my work because he felt it undermined his.

At Harris, I built a client profitability model that turned the average retail customer into one of the bank's most profitable segments. All boring stuff, I can admit that. However, with Hope on my mind, I needed to distract myself with exactly that flavor of boring. The functional processes involved with my job mostly helped.

Until the phone rang. When I looked at the call display, I debated whether it was worth speaking to Gordon at all.

At last, I picked up. "Gordo—"

He didn't let me finish, but I blamed that on his kids. "You are a fucking moron." He took care to enunciate each word individually. Gordon had time for these little games. At the moment, I needed boring.

I sat straighter in my chair. "She called you, didn't she? I knew she would."

He chuckled on the other end of the line, and I swear I heard him shaking his head at me. "Hope?"

This was a good sign. The grin that crept onto my face felt good, like the sun coming out after an extended period of hiding between the raindrops. "What did she tell you?"

A long, tired sigh. I had heard it from him before. "It wasn't Hope, Cam. Riley called me. But this? This I needed to hear for myself."

"Oh." I slumped forward, grabbed a pen and started twirling it between my fingers.

"Are you sure you're normal? What you're doing, it's…" Another sigh, and I shifted in my chair from the sudden discomfort. "…it's damaging. This isn't the kind of stuff that heals. It's not a scar that you can make her feel pretty about."

"Listen, I have to run, Gordo."

"What would you have done if Hope wanted to see the condo? I know you; I fucking know what you did. I even think I know what you're up to with this."

"I need to get back to work," I told him, sighing without caring if he heard my impatience.

"No, what you need is to have lunch with me."

"Can't." I checked the data on my computer screen. "Too much to get done."

"Nah, you're having lunch with me today. I'm going to be

downtown anyway. Melinda wants to redo the wills. She gets like this after my expensive trips with the boys."

"She should," I said, noticing that I had just received a new email.

"What the fuck does that mean? You're on my team, don't forget that."

"And you're supposed to be on mine," I reminded him, equaling his irritation. "But I can't have lunch today, no matter whose team you're on."

"Bullshit. And I *am* on your team. You're just too fucking stupid to see it."

"We'll chat later, Gordo." I clicked on my inbox icon and found the message that had caught my attention. It was sent by hmcmanus@probstllc.com.

"Yes, we will," Gordo said. "Call me once you get home."

"Uh huh." I absently dropped the phone back into the base and clicked on her email.

> Hey. Sorry about last night. I'd like to see you at lunch today and talk. I have so much to tell you, and I can't have another night of sleeplessness. Please say you're free…
>
> Hope

I hammered a quick response: *See you at 1pm in the lobby.*

Within seconds, she replied with an even shorter: *OK.*

It was officially our second date in as many days.

PRESENT DAY

CHAPTER 14

8:20 AM

Having been faced with the prospect of losing her forever several times already, I know a thing or two about showing up for the moment. This moment. So when I spot Hope among the crowd of commuters pouring out of the train station, I take that deep breath you take before jumping off a rocky cliff into the uncertain waters below.

"I told you, I'm too busy," she greets me as I fall into stride next to her. The pulsing vein on her neck tells me that there is definitely room for negotiation here. Some, anyway. "I'm sorry, Cameron."

"Let's walk together." All part of the plan, I remind myself to stick to the plan.

"You and I both know that your boss isn't your biggest fan right now. Maybe you should turn around and go home before you get too close to the office and your boss sees you."

I reach for her hand, but she snaps it out of my reach. Nice. Real mature.

"You need to go home," she continues. Her inability to keep

quiet for more than a few seconds tells me everything I need to know.

"I'm sorry. I can't let you leave this time," I say with a tone of empathy, like I'm the teacher who can't let my favorite student get away with cheating. "It's not going to happen."

She drops her head back and laughs so loudly that the people ahead of us actually turn around to see what someone could find so funny before eight-thirty in the morning on the last Friday before Labor Day weekend.

"I'm serious, Hope. Real serious."

"And you're seriously going to be unemployed in three more blocks. Don't put that on my shoulders, goob."

"You talk like an M & M, you know that, right?" I hide my grin by scratching my jawline.

"You talk like an imbecile."

"Hard candy shell on the outside—"

She rolls her eyes. "Sweet chocolate on the inside, I get it—"

"Followed by nuts," I add, "because we're talking about peanut M & M's."

She hits me hard, but her lips finally curl into the first sign of defeat. "You're a certifiable goob."

We walk half a block. It kills me because this silence feels like sand slipping through my fingers.

"Listen," I continue. "You talk about that story like it's us."

"It *is* us, Cameron," she insists, her face tightening. "And like Oliver and Olivia, our timing is wrong. Your being here is wrong." She shakes her head. "Like Oliver, you had your chance with me, but you blew it."

"You blew it, too," I blurt out, then hate myself for walking into this trap, yet again. "But I'm here now, and I'm not letting you go without a fight. I'm going to fight fucking hard, even if that means hauling you off over my shoulder."

"I'd like to see you try that."

"Sounds like a dare."

"More like a threat." Deep sigh. "And I'm serious. I can't miss work today."

"You *can* miss work today," I promise, walking ahead of her and turning around to get into her face a little. "Not only can you miss work, but you can miss your flight next week when you're supposed to move out West."

"Cameron…"

"Hope, that senior citizen you're engaged to doesn't deserve you. You know that just as well as I do. And not because you're way better than him, but because your heart doesn't belong there."

She groans. "You're a cardiologist all of a sudden?"

I start reaching for her hand again, but stop myself. It's too soon. "Look at me, Hope."

"No way, Cameron!" she squawks. "You're pushing it!"

"Oliver and Olivia and that story you just can't let go of, it's all about seizing the moments while you have them. Those two people exist, right?"

She shakes her head, but I can see that the gears are turning in her mind. "It's all made up. Emma and some accountant started this thing…"

"And how did things turn out for Emma? Did she and this other guy end up together?" I wait a few seconds for a response that never comes. We both know the answer to my question, so it doesn't surprise me when Hope stays quiet. Which is great because now isn't the time for the two of us to get involved in a long, drawn out dissertation regarding some story about two people who couldn't get their shit together. Now is the time for me to reach for her hand and pull her aside so she'll look at me, once and for all.

In one ninja-swift motion out of a Fred Astaire routine, I grab her wrist and wheel her out of the flow of pedestrian traffic, twirling her into the doorway that belongs to an emergency exit for one of the older buildings.

She tries not to laugh at the sudden spontaneity of my motion, frowning and giving me that faux pissed-off glare of hers instead. "Cameron!"

"Hope, shut up for a minute. Just look at me." She stays quiet, so while I catch my breath, I nudge her chin upward with my hand. "Please. Just look into my eyes." She complies, and I smile softly. "There, how's that? Better?"

She hesitates before her shoulders slouch. "I can't do this."

"You *can* do this," I insist. This is my last fucking card, and I have to play it. It's now or never. "We *need* this day. Just the two of us. I've made all of these arrangements for today, and I swear, if it's the last thing I do for you, for the woman I love more than any human should be allowed to love, that's fine." I reach out and nudge her chin again, forcing her to stare straight into my eyes. "Hope, please." I motion at the space between us. "This is the worst kind of love out there."

I can practically feel her heart pounding, and all I'm holding is her hand. I know this because my chest wants to burst, too.

"Cameron," she whispers, but I can tell she's given up. She will call in sick today.

"This love," I tell her, "is the kind that destroys people. Give me this one day, Hope. This final day. If you give me this, and you still get on that plane next week…"

"I *am* getting on that plane," she says, her voice about as convincing as a two-year-old telling you he didn't shit himself despite the sagging diaper around his waist.

"…then I will give you the freedom you've asked for." I release her hand and place mine over my left breast. "I will stop fighting for you. I will let go. Forever."

Her pretty hazel eyes dance across my face as she calculates her risks like any good accountant would.

I make one last plea. "Hope, this is *our* story. Let's write it together."

At last, she gives a long sigh and shakes her head at me. "Damn you, Cameron."

I hand her my phone. "I've programmed your boss's number. Just press SEND and you're set."

She slaps my hand away. "You better pull through and give me that freedom once today is over."

"I promise." And the promise I make to my heart is that I won't let go again.

Shaking her head again, she reaches into her bag and retrieves her phone. I watch her scroll through her contact list and find the right number before pressing the phone to the side of her face. "Cameron…" she sighs.

"Should've just used my phone. We've already wasted a minute, at least." A minute to those in the crowd could mean a crazy market fluctuation, a late slip, a lost paycheck. A minute waiting for Hope meant more wasted moments, memories that would never happen.

"*Shh!*" she scolds me. And then, "Hiya, Ian? Sorry to do this on a Friday before the long weekend, but I'm really not feeling well."

two months ago

CHAPTER 15

Seeing Hope in the lobby at 1:03 that afternoon, I felt my world quake. She strode with absolute confidence, unwilling give up the slightest indication of her true thoughts or feelings, while I struggled to keep my shit together. It didn't help that she was the only image of perfection I had ever known.

"Sorry about last night," I said, shrugging once she was close enough to hear me. "How crazy did Matt get once you got home?"

She waved me to a bench in the lobby, which could mean nothing but bad news. Not a stroll in the park, not an invitation to a nearby restaurant. A shitty bench with all of these people around us. I sat down, but she remained standing. Yup, bad news.

"You're not hungry?" I asked.

"Cameron, please," she said, the wariness in her tone signaling defeat, surrender. "I just want to apologize. I'm not hungry, I'm tired."

"Food will give you energy."

At last, a half-smile tickled the edge of her mouth, followed by a sigh, which essentially nullified any sign of her softening shell.

"My condo is a couple blocks away." I pointed out the window, remembering the diner I passed yesterday en route to the Bat Cave. "I've got some tasty left overs I could reheat…"

She massaged her temples, closing her eyes for a moment before snapping them back to me. Her resolve returned with a ferocity I knew only as Hope. "Cameron, this needs to stop."

"Lunch is an important meal, Hope. Why won't you let me feed you?"

"Not the lunch, goob," she said, but no smirk or other hint of lightheartedness reached the surface like I had expected. "All of this crazy shit. About us. I'm sorry, but I can't keep doing this."

"Doing what?"

She placed a hand on my shoulder and gave me the sternest stare I had ever known from her. "Matt was right. I need you to understand something. You and I need to stop. You need to move on. I need to move on. It's not fair to Matt that you and I have reconnected."

"You're moving away soon enough, so what's the harm?"

"It's not fair to anyone. You shouldn't risk your marriage with Riley. You and I, we had our shot. We missed it. It's time to let go and move on." She gave me a curt nod, then turned to walk away, but I seized her wrist and pulled her back.

"I've still got something like fifty minutes before I'm expected back from lunch," I said. I tried to keep the desperation out of my voice. "Let's talk about this."

She shook her head. "I'm sorry, Cameron. I need to go." She yanked her wrist free, pulling it so hard that I almost fell off the bench. Her strength surprised me. I had forgotten just how strong she could be. I covered up my fumble by standing and following her to the elevators.

"Then I'm coming with you," I said.

"No, you're not." She hit the button for the elevators, then stepped aboard the first one.

I followed her in.

"You won't get past the hallway without a special key fob. What are you thinking?"

"I'm thinking you're full of shit, Hope." I meant it, too. "I'm thinking you're working really hard at pushing me away, testing me. And nobody works that hard at something that should be easy. Which tells me it's not something you want. You don't want me to disappear; you want me to keep fighting, to never let go. Because if we weren't meant to be together, pushing me away wouldn't be so hard, would it?"

The elevator stopped. I followed Hope into a hallway. She walked toward a single doorway at the end of that hall.

"Hope, give me forty-five minutes," I begged. "Let's talk this through."

She reached the door and turned around. I saw that her eyes were a little moist. This was *not* fun for her. How could I have ever questioned that? She kept her voice low, almost a whisper. "This isn't fair to Matt. He's a good man. He's always there for me. And I love him."

"He's wrong for you."

She frowned, as if I had just sprinkled cold water on her face. "*This* is wrong, Cameron. You need to go."

I studied her eyes as they bore into mine, scarring my soul. I felt fully vulnerable right then, but it didn't matter; she had seen all of me already…she owned me.

"Okay," I said. "You win." When she started to turn away, I blurted that I love her. "I won't stop," I elaborated. "But if it makes it easier for you to think that our meeting the other day at Panera wasn't some motion of fate or destiny, then you're crazy."

She froze, her back to me. "You need to leave now, Cameron." And then she seemed to remember what she was doing and used her special access fob to get inside the office where she worked. And when she disappeared inside, I thought of the other time she had left without a glance back.

Cold, yes.

But this time, I stood there for a beat before realizing the truth behind her message. All of this bullshit with wanting to see me, wanting to tell me to fuck off to my face…it could mean only one thing.

She still loved me.

After getting back to my desk, I sent Hope the following email:

> Hey, no worries about the miscommunication today at lunch. I know you're tired and didn't mean anything by what you said. How about we reschedule lunch for tomorrow? And we can actually eat something this time?
>
> - Cam

I waited all day for a response that never came. I even stayed at work a little later than normal. By 5:30, I felt Newman's dickhead presence behind me. I rotated in my chair and stared at him, curious about the sneer on his face.

"You're not getting in-lieu time, Cam," he said.

I gave an understanding nod. "It's not what I'm after."

The edges of his lips began to curl upward, the double chin somehow enhanced in his moment of personal victory. "This doesn't provide you any job security, either."

I made a show of checking the watch on my wrist. "It's half an hour, Newman. I'm only doing what I always do."

He gave a fake chuckle. "What would that be?"

"An exceptional job."

The insincere camaraderie melted off his face. If he could've grown demonic horns out the top of his head, this would've been their birthing moment.

"I don't expect that you've gone through the single-purchase report," I said. "So I'm writing my recommendations right now. In plain, third-grade English," I added. "With pretty pie charts and colorful profitability projections, and—"

"Go home, Cam," Newman growled, having burned through what little patience he had left. "White-gloved princesses like you don't survive in the trenches. It's the hard-working, back-breaking, middle-management types like me who make sure you and your big-boy friends upstairs don't bring the rest of our company down." He turned and walked away, sneering down the length of his nose like he owned the world.

"Maybe you're wrong about me, Newman," I called out after him.

"Not a chance," he said, his back to me. "I'm never wrong."

"There's always a first," I said.

"Not this time," he huffed as he left the 45th floor work area and entered the elevator lobby.

Shaking my head at his ridiculousness, I returned to the computer. I checked my inbox first. When I saw that Hope still hadn't responded, I refocused on the report and absent-mindedly completed my write up. By 6:15, I was all finished, fired it off to Newman, then packed up and left for the night.

CHAPTER 16

I decided on the twenty-minute walk home. It was a slightly longer commute than taking the subway, but it afforded me some time to clear my head for what I imagined awaited me at the condo.

I cut across West Wacker and walked North on Michigan Avenue, always amazed by the clusters of tourists. It never really mattered what time of year it was, they came here like it was Times Square, spending more money at these high-end shops than they would if they travelled just a little farther off this beaten path.

But mostly, I watched the couples. I watched them holding hands, smiling at each other, talking, kissing, and that sight begged the question: were Riley and I like them? Did we hold hands, smile, talk, and kiss like these people did? Of course we put on the show of a happy couple, but there was something more when I saw these complete strangers doing those things. But these people lacked something. They lacked the therapeutic, clinical affection that Riley and I shared.

To say I felt a little lonely in my young marriage would be an understatement. All the affection and sap-inspired togetherness on Michigan Avenue was making me think of just one other person, and she hadn't responded to my email. I wasn't delusional enough to ignore just how pathetic I was to cling to this idea that Hope and I would be together someday. It was the most insane belief in the world, and I fully accepted that.

I made my left on Huron and noticed how quickly all of that love and togetherness dissipated after a block, and how completely gone it was by the time I reached my building, where the doorman gave me a salaried smile and opened the lobby door.

I rode the elevator to the 30th floor, keeping my head down as I walked the quiet hallway to my door at the end. As I slid the key into the lock and eased the door open, I sensed her behind me. I caught myself stopping and wanting to look back, but recovered quickly and simply entered the unit like I hadn't noticed her at all.

"Hey, Riley, I'm home," I called out to the emptiness, easing the door shut. The moment the door latched, I pressed my face to the peephole to see if I had been correct.

In the fish-eye view, I saw her approaching me, my unit. Her strut was as confident as it had been earlier today at lunch. I waited. And it hurt. I felt sick and happy and sad and angry and pained and triumphant, and everything else she ever made me feel.

Once she was close enough to raise her fist to knock, I yanked the door open and pulled her inside, throwing her back up against the wall.

"Look at me," I begged against her thrashing. "Look at me!"

"Cameron!" she yelled, hammering me with her balled fists, but that rage didn't last long as I reached up and took her face with my hands. "Stop! Don't!"

I tilted my head and erased the distance between our faces. "Look—"

"Stop it! Don't!" She kept pounding my chest, angry and hurt. "Don't you dare! Don't you fucking—"

But when I pressed my lips to hers, all she did was melt into me, wrapping her legs around my waist and locking her arms around my neck.

She loved me. Just like I had loved her all of this time, like I would always love her. She loved me back without saying the words.

PRESENT DAY

CHAPTER 17

8:56 AM

Terzo Piano is the well-known and popular dining room located within the Art Institute of Chicago. The chef lives in the same building as I do, and some of Gordon's executive friends are or were big donors to the AIC (along with the Clinton family). So last week, when I first started planning this sick day, I made two phone calls in one day and cornered the Chef in my lobby the next. Technically, the restaurant only served lunch during the week, but those phone calls had worked wonders.

"Where are we going?" Hope asks as we stroll across the pedestrian bridge. Halfway to the other side, I stop her and point straight down Monroe into the belly of downtown Chicago.

"It doesn't matter, because we're not there."

"Cameron, are you kidding me? You brought me up here to tell me that?" She slaps at my wrist. "I hope your boss is looking here right this instant."

I snuggle closer to her and breathe in her coconut scent, but she shoves me away. "I hope so, too," I admit. "Then I'll have an excuse to chase you out west if you still get on that plane."

"I *am* getting on that plane, goob! And you promised to leave me alone once I do."

Saying nothing else, I place my hand on the lower part of her back and nudge her forward, continuing across the bridge toward the AIC's Modern Wing.

"What are we doing? The museum? Really?" She frowns at me.

I try to put a finger on her lips to shush her, but she slaps my hand away. So much for foreplay. "You'll see."

As we reach the glass doors, a waitress in a white shirt and a black skirt puts on a smile and opens the door for us. "Nice to see you, Cam."

She gives me a polite nod as I escort Hope into the restaurant. I glance over at her to see how impressed she is. On a scale of one to ten—ten being absolutely dumbfounded—I place her at a one, absolutely unimpressed.

"Right this way," the waitress says, steering us past the reception counter to a wide-open, white room. Normally, this space would have a variety of tables positioned throughout the vast floor. Then again, Terzo Piano normally doesn't open until eleven during the week. Instead of its regular scattering of dining tables, there is only one table here today.

A white one, with two white chairs and white table settings.

Squarely in the middle.

I glance at Hope a second time to see if the needle has

budged from that one to something higher, like a twenty.

"So?" I ask, because it doesn't look like she's really all that absolutely dumbfounded.

"Am I supposed to be taking pictures?" she responds.

Okay. I start laughing because what she just said was a little funny, but I'm also disappointed she doesn't get the message just yet. "Let's sit down." Maybe it will sink in for her then.

The waitress holds Hope's chair out for her, then presents us with orange juice and offers coffee or tea. I decline, but Hope motions for the tea. When the waitress disappears, she leans over the table to get closer to me, and if her crimped forehead is any indication, she's a little confused.

"What is all of this supposed to mean, Cameron?"

I lean forward, toying with the napkin. Here goes. "Two months ago—"

She presses her back into her seat, shaking her head and cutting me off. "No, no, no. This is *not* about what happened two months ago."

I think about it for a minute. "Okay, you're right. It's not just two months ago. It's three years ago, it's ten years ago, it's since the beginning of time for us. That's what this is, isn't it?"

She gives an elaborate wave to the nearly empty white space. "If you're trying to impress me—"

"I knew it!"

"Knew what?" she asks, sincerely unimpressed.

"I knew that you were impressed."

She laughs at me. "That's the point. Because I'm *not* impressed. Taking me out of work to buy me breakfast at some restaurant you paid off with your big-shot connections and big-shot severance package—"

"What are you suggesting, Hope?" I can hear my voice getting tighter and the high-pitched words echoing off the walls and tall ceiling like a ping-pong ball in a concert hall.

She rolls her eyes, and, just like that, we've fallen back into that push-and-pull existence that we know all too well.

"Matt never bought me," she confides. "You think it's about his money, but I'm not something he picked off some shelf and bought."

"You're right, he hasn't bought you. If anything, he's renting you," I mumble.

"You're an asshole."

"And you're in denial, Hope." I point back over my shoulder, the tension rising into my shoulders. "Two months ago wasn't goodbye. You showed up at *my* place after you told me to fuck off at lunch, remember?"

"Stop it." She crosses her legs and pulls her attention away.

"You kissed me, and it was fucking perfect and everything that followed was—"

She throws her napkin on the table and pushes her chair out. "Stop it, or I'm walking away. And this time I won't show up to apologize."

I hold my hands up in defeat, letting out a long breath.

"Please don't. This isn't supposed to be like this, Hope."

"Then what's it supposed to be, Cameron?"

I stare at the table for what feels like an eternity. *Where's the fucking tea already?* When I look up to Hope's hardened face, I see that maybe it—this—really is over. That seems to be the trend for me these days.

"What's it supposed to be?" she asks again, tapping her foot on the floor.

I take a big gulp of air, building up courage. Fast. "Three years ago, I fucked up. I fucked up when I didn't come after you."

"We're not talking about three years ago, Cameron. We're talking about now. About what now is supposed to be like at this fancy little dining space you've rented for me."

"For us," I correct her.

"Semantics." She softens a little. "So what's it supposed to be like now?"

Hope's tea arrives, affording me a bit of time to refocus my energy, to think of something brilliant to say because she's truly not seeing the importance of our breakfast here. I watch her pour a packet of fake sugar and 2% milk into her tea, stirring it with a hand that trembles just enough for me to notice.

When she brings her attention back to me before lifting the steaming cup to her lips, I tell her what now is supposed to be like. "It's supposed to be like we promised it would. Before we even left for college."

"But those days are gone and dead, Cameron," she sighs.

"Just like three years ago, just like two months ago. It can never be like that, like we promised. So now what are you left with?"

Easy. I tap the table once to hammer my point home. "This moment. And if you think I'm going to let go of this moment ever again, you're wrong. I'm never letting go. I'm never letting go of you, Hope."

With that promise, her eyes turn into the magic of shooting stars, but it doesn't last long because the waitress returns, this time with our breakfast.

The promise of never letting go isn't wasted, though. It lingers between us, and I know she'll think about it for the rest of our day together. Maybe even the rest of her life if she doesn't tell Matt she's leaving him.

THREE YEARS AGO

CHAPTER 18

While I set the dinner table, I came face-to-face with an interesting paradox. I had made two promises—one to the woman who was singing in the shower upstairs, after a long week of being underpaid and abused by arrogant white-collar mind-rapists; the other to the woman who stood outside my townhouse in the rain, watching me from the shadows of the neighbor's minivan. But keeping one of them meant breaking the other.

How bizarre, I thought, noticing her pale face in the darkness. I stepped away from the table-setting to see if I had hallucinated the sight of Hope McManus after all of these years. How bizarre that keeping one promise meant breaking another, and here was one of those promises standing outside the home I owned with my fiancée.

"Holy shit," I breathed, staring out the large window and straight into Hope's eyes. I raised a hand to her, almost like a wave, but she only stared back at me. Because of the rain, I couldn't tell if she was crying or angry or a freaking ghost, really.

"Cam!" Riley called from upstairs.

"What?" I yelled back, but I refused to pull my eyes from the sight of Hope, *my Hope*.

"Do we have time for a quickie? What's left on the timer?"

Shit. A quickie with Hope standing outside?

"No!" I said.

"Okay, I'll be right down," Riley promised. "It smells amazing!"

Fuck, even worse.

"Wait, wait!" I shouted back. "I'll be right up."

I didn't know if there was twenty minutes or twenty seconds left on the timer for whatever it was I had placed in the oven. All I knew was that if Riley came downstairs, I would have to pull my stare away from Hope. And I also knew that once I broke this stare between us, she would disappear.

Again.

"Hurry up!" Riley shouted. "I'm already wet, and I'm gonna get started without you! Damn, I'm fucking horny tonight!"

"Uh huh," I mumbled, raising my hand to Hope again. Except this time I gave her the "one minute" sign, which probably looked like the "this is my pointer finger" sign as well.

Backing away from the front window, I hurried to the front door, taking my eyes off her for less than five seconds as I searched for my shoes, then decided to bypass any footwear because it would take too long to tie the laces. Then I ran outside to find exactly what I had expected.

She was gone.

Our exclusive, executive community had our row of townhomes facing another row, with a common laneway between us. It led to a mound of pretty landscaping and a gazebo that apparently justified the $500 per month in common fees. I searched that laneway, looked up and down. On the down search, I caught sight of Hope running away. Not toward the gazebo, which would've been the easiest thing.

"Hope!" I yelled, then launched into a sprint after her. I pumped my legs harder than I had in the past few weeks because I had been too busy at Harris to even see the gym, let alone start any kind of workout. But I was quick, and I was gaining on her as she steered off the grounds and onto the busy four-lane street.

"Hope!" I begged

"No!" she yelled, glancing back to see how close I was getting.

"Stop for a minute! Please! I'm gonna fucking die here!"

"Then fuck off and die, Cameron!" she screamed.

Once I was close enough, I lunged at her and tackled her to the drenched grass next to the community center. The lights from the indoor pool where old people did water-cise activities flooded onto us. I glanced inside the pool area, but nobody seemed to notice the shoeless young man who had just taken down the soaking wet young woman outside their group exercise class.

"Hope, stop!" I begged her.

But she didn't stop; she kept squirming and fighting in my arms, even as I held her in this tight spooning position.

"Shit, will you just stop already?" I screamed, then kissed the side of her face because I missed her. Oh, fuck, did I ever miss her, the taste of her face on my lips, but I also didn't know what else to do.

That kiss did it. The ferocity of her squirming and fighting lightened.

I kissed her again and again and again, until she turned her lips to mine and rotated her body so that she lay underneath my weight on the spongy grass. The rain pelted my back as we made out like two rabid teenagers whose parents wouldn't lend them their cars so they could screw in the dry privacy of a backseat.

When I pulled back from Hope's reciprocated kisses, I realized that I was pinning her wrists above her head, and she had wrapped her legs around my waist.

"Look at us," I said, and we both burst into crazy laughter.

"I missed you, Cameron," she panted. "Shit."

"Hope, what are you doing here?"

She sighed, turning her face toward the swimming pool window and aiming her stare on the activity inside like it offered the answer to the meaning of life.

"Not this."

CHAPTER 19

Returning to the townhouse, drenched and barefoot, I didn't exactly know what to expect from Riley. I stood on the front porch for a few moments, wondering for a second if Riley had managed to get off before the timer buzzed on the oven, then turned the doorknob and stepped inside. I braced myself for the worst, but was surprised when she stepped into the foyer, wearing a bathrobe and carrying a glass of wine. She simply looked me up and down with a questioning look on her face.

"Where the fuck were you?" she asked with a hiss, opening her bathrobe just enough to reveal that she wore nothing underneath. For the first time in forever, the sight of Riley's naked body did nothing to arouse me. Normally, her beauty alone had an insta-hard-on effect that lasted hours. Not tonight.

I chuckled and tried to step past her, but she stopped me.

"So? Where were you, Cam?" She bit her fingernail.

"In the basement," I lied. "Where the fuck does it look like I was?"

My tone offended her enough that she stepped back and tightened the robe. I moved into the kitchen for some food because that was what a normal person would do.

"How was the ham?" I asked.

"It was a roasted chicken," Riley answered. "And I'm going to bed."

"Goodnight," I breathed once she was gone, then found the roasted chicken and dumped a bit onto my plate. How could I have forgotten that it was chicken? Damn, seeing Hope had seriously messed with my head.

I walked to the table with my plate. Seeing as tonight had been the first time that I spent time with Hope in roughly seven years, it made sense why I was a little disoriented, confused, whatever. The loss of appetite surprised me, though, as I toyed with my dinner—two thin slices off the breast along with a spoonful of vegetables—and wondered why I had dumped so much on my plate. I wasn't hungry. At all.

Yet upstairs, Riley was probably waiting for me to come and kiss her ass, apologize for the tone and the words and sarcasm. Then start sucking on her toes while holding her ankle with one hand and massaging her clit with the other, exactly what she had been expecting before dinner.

I moved my eyes from the plate to the stairwell leading to that clit-massage, then back to the plate. This wasn't the type of decision that should confuse someone who wasn't even married yet, but I couldn't decide whether I wanted the chicken or my fiancée's nipples in my mouth.

I settled on the chicken. It was just a little easier that way.

CHAPTER 20

The first time I told Gordo about Hope was that Monday morning after dry humping her on the grass outside the community center in the pouring rain. Both Gordo and I had great jobs at Harris—he as an Executive VP, me as a Senior Manager. We had no idea what awaited us in the coming week. So in the most general terms, we absolutely loved life at this bank. A lot.

That Monday morning, I stopped at Gordo's office en route to mine, and he knew right away that something fantastic had happened.

"No fucking way," he said, stepping away from the mini-putting green and dropping onto his leather sofa overlooking the Chicago River. "You tried anal, didn't you? Jeez, man, what did you think?" He made a fucking motion with his hips and wiggled his eyebrows at me.

"It wasn't anal," I said, the smile melting off my face courtesy of the bile rising up my throat. "That's fucking gross this early in the morning; why would you think that? Of all things, Gordo…"

Laughing, Gordon completely ignored the severity of my mood and sat straighter on the sofa. Keeping his back rigid, he ran his hands down the sides of his mouth. "This looks serious, Cam."

I nodded.

"Are you leaving Harris? You know there's nothing better out there right now. These banks are just getting back into hiring. And even then…"

I shook my head, grinning at the ridiculousness of his suggestion. "No, nothing like that. I can't leave this job. You know that. I love this place."

"Then what is it?" he asked. "If it's not anal and it's not the career, then I fucking give up."

Deep breath. "Well, when I was high school, I promised this girl that we'd be together forever."

Gordon howled, clapping his hands. "Are you serious? This is turning out to be a pretty awesome Monday! Let me guess, you gave this girl a promise ring, didn't you?" He laughed some more.

"Well, we obviously didn't end up together. Because I hooked up with Riley after that first semester at Northwestern."

He became serious again at the mention of my fiancée. "Yeah, Riley's got that kind of body, that I can-fuck-this-forever kind of body, and the blonde hair of fucking wet dreams." He pulled his attention from whatever semi-pornographic images of my fiancée had just occupied his mind and looked at my face instead. "I'd say things turned out okay for you, Cam."

I winced.

"Was that offside? I mean, I just meant to say that Riley's hot, it's not exactly a crime to fall for the pretty girl."

I shrugged. "Wasn't offside, Gordo. But a promise was a

promise, and instead of taking her calls or answering her emails, I just disappeared."

He chuckled again. "You know how many guys make high-school promises?"

"This was a pretty big promise," I said, shrugging and wincing at the same time.

He just shook his head. "I can't tell you how many times I promised to marry girls at parties, just for a blow job. And that was just last weekend!" He frowned when my eyes widened. "Kidding about last weekend, by the way. So, why are you thinking about this bullshit on a Monday morning anyway? Don't you have a big presentation to the C-team on how we're going to improve retail-client profitability?"

I took another deep breath and stared down at the putting green and the half-dozen balls assembled at the cup. "Because this girl showed up on Friday. No warning or anything. She just showed up, and I haven't stopped thinking about her since." When I raised my attention to Gordon's eyes, I told him what was really troubling me. "Now I don't know if I should be marrying Riley next month."

CHAPTER 21

I worked late every night that week, lying to Riley about some made-up client-behavior reports because I just couldn't stop thinking about Hope. And being at home made me antsy in an ADHD way.

Gordon knew it, too. Each night before he left at seven, he stopped at my office, leaning on the doorframe with his laptop bag hanging off his shoulder. "Is this distraction supposed to show up tonight?" he asked. It was the same question he had been asking since Monday. Even tonight, one week since last Friday's run-in with Hope, it was the same thing.

"Yes," I answered with a convincing nod, but Gordo could somehow tell that I was lying.

"Really? She *told* you she would show up? Every day this week, or just tonight?"

"She'll show up," I told him, not really in a mood to play his games. "And when she does, I don't know how it will turn out."

Shaking his head, he let out a deep sigh. "Crazy week we've had, huh? Monday, you were talking about promises you made to some girl in high school. Now we're sitting here wondering about the promises our bosses have made to us about the security of our jobs. Well, that's what the rest of us on the floor are wondering about. And you're up here on a Friday night, thinking about the first girl you ever fucked."

"She wasn't the first. But it was a promise, Gordo. Can we drop it?"

He waved at the emptiness behind him. "How many times have we been promised safety and security, dude? You know, we survived that financial crisis, we fought for our fucking lives, raping and pillaging at every fucking turn because of a promise. So do you really want to talk about what that word means? I've got two kids and two nannies at home; I rely on promises to get me from week to week, to keep my wife smiling and those kids happy."

I shook my head. "Yeah, that's exactly what I mean. It's that happiness you're talking about. Hope is my promise, and I was hers. We fit together so well."

Either he didn't hear me or he didn't care to listen. Gordon just kept talking like I hadn't said anything. "But just like this bullshit with Harris head office, Cam, what the fuck happened? Just like I've been sitting in my office since that meeting Wednesday morning, wondering why they've suddenly changed their minds about the great work all of us do on this floor. I have to wonder why you didn't honor *your* promise to this Hope girl. Why did you disappear in the first place? I mean, all week you've been bitching and moaning about how much you miss her, and now you're contemplating bailing on your wedding to Riley, which is a matrimonial promise, isn't it?"

I had no response for him as he pushed away from the doorframe, shaking his head at me.

"Just like these cocksuckers broke their promise to me about how safe and secure we all are, you broke yours to this girl." He let that sink in, and then added, "You broke your promise to Hope, and there was a reason for that. Don't forget it before you go and ruin the rest of your life, and Riley's life, on something that was never meant to be."

He walked away, but before he was completely out of sight, I called after him. "Hey, Gordo!"

"Go home to your fiancée, Cam!" he yelled back from somewhere down the hall.

"Have a good weekend," I mumbled, turning to my computer and powering down.

It was time to leave, time to find Riley and forget about this craziness of the past week. I decided on picking up flowers, some salts for the tub, and that Canadian wine we discovered a few weeks ago. Maybe she could slip back into that bathrobe, too. And this time, I wouldn't be putting anything in the oven. I'd be fucking her instead.

CHAPTER 22

I made it halfway through the Harris Building lobby when I noticed the tall brunette in the dark corner next to the revolving doors, watching me. Hope. I knew it from her presence alone; I didn't have to see her face or the color of her hair or smell her perfume or coconut shampoo to know; I could tell because I knew how I *felt* whenever she was near.

"Working late?" she asked, stepping toward me. "I was afraid your security guard was going to kick me out."

The stupid-big smile that twisted onto my face crushed my determination from earlier. Riley? Salts for the tub? Wine and fucking to the point where we have to change the sheets before bed?

Wait, Riley who?

"So what's her name, Cameron?" Hope asked as she pushed into the revolving doors, but they refused to budge. She pushed harder, and I just watched, holding back laughter. Awkward.

"They lock the doors after hours," I informed her. "You can push as hard as you want, but they won't budge."

She stepped back into the lobby, smirking and shaking her head at me. She wasn't really embarrassed, but if anyone else had seen her, I knew she would have blushed. "Goob! Were you going to let me make an idiot of myself all night?"

"No, it didn't take more than a few seconds for you to do that all on your own. So how long have you been waiting for me?"

"Since four-thirty. I didn't know what time you left for the day, so I stood there and watched, waiting for you. Now I have to pee."

I chuckled. "I didn't think you believed in fighting for love. This is a new side to you."

She punched me in the shoulder, hard. "What's your wife's name already?"

"Riley," I answered, rubbing my shoulder. "And she's just my fiancée. At least until next month when we're supposed to get married in Wisconsin."

Now it was Hope's turn to chuckle. "I didn't know you believed in marriage. This is a new side to you, Cameron."

"I…uh…" I brushed a hand through my hair, remembering how I had been questioning the marriage thing all week since seeing Hope. If Riley's and my relationship was based on love—the real and tangible kind that keeps you smiling every morning when you wake up next to that person, the kind that allows you to conceive and raise children in the best environment possible—should Hope have had such a profound impact when we were this close to my wedding day? Now I wondered whether marrying Riley was the right thing to do.

"I've never been to Chicago," she said. "Deep dish pizza?"

I felt a little dizzy; she seemed to be coming at me from a million different angles. "Yes. We can eat. Sure."

I used my access card to release the lock on the exit door. The warm air and city sounds washed over us the moment we stepped outside. I took a deep breath, then glanced over at Hope again, just to make sure this was real, not some dream or fantasy. I couldn't believe she was here. Again.

"What are you doing in Chicago, anyway?" I had to ask.

She gave me a threatening glare, then shook her head. "I'm in the same boat as you."

"Facing certain unemployment?"

"Huh?" She glared at me sideways.

"Nevermind." I turned north on Wells. "It's a bit of a hike to Gino's East, but you'll love it. How long are you in Chicago?"

I felt her hand slip into mine, but I pulled away. Riley knew a lot of people in Chicago; I didn't want her to hear rumors from someone else when we had so little time between now and our wedding day. I couldn't crush her like that. But in the process of protecting Riley's heart, I noticed that a part of Hope's crumbled away.

She changed the subject again. "I have to pee. How far is this place?"

"Fifteen minutes if you can hold it that long."

We walked in silence for a few blocks. At Ohio, Hope pointed toward the golden arches a city block to the east, the original McDonald's. "Holy shit!"

"We're real close, unless you're going to piss your pants."

"Shut up and keep walking," she said, poking me in the kidneys to keep my feet going. "I'm only here for a few more nights."

"That's too bad." Like if my heart just stopped beating.

"Why's that, Cameron?" she snapped. "Were you hoping I'd come to your wedding?"

At Gino's East, they seated us at a booth, but Hope walked straight to the bathrooms in the back, her legs so tight together that, from behind, she appeared to be walking on one leg. The waiter came, and I ordered our drinks. A Coke for me and an iced tea for Hope—almost like we were still dating before college, still in love, and still blissfully oblivious to the complications that a bullet-proof, five-year promise would have on our relationship.

What am I doing here?

When Hope returned, sliding into the booth across from me, I told her what I had done—ordered her an iced tea—and her lips twitched like she might be flirting with the idea of a smile. "I've missed you, Cameron."

I nodded. "I gathered that from last week's encounter in the rain."

"I know you missed me more." Her face lit up at the memory.

Last Friday night, after we finished making out on the grass, we retreated to the nearest bus shelter and talked. I told her where I worked, told her to come find me so we could talk some more. On Monday, I had expected her to show up, but by today, despite my confidence with Gordon, I hadn't held much hope that I would ever see her again.

"Why did you disappear, Cameron? I called, I emailed, and nothing." She seemed a little hurt about that, and I couldn't blame her.

"I met Riley," I told her, point-blank.

"She's pretty," Hope admitted sadly and quickly; she didn't seem to want to hear more about Riley right now. "Very pretty."

The waiter came with our drinks, and we ordered a small deep-dish pizza.

I watched Hope pucker her lips around the straw and take a long pull from the glass, her pretty hazel eyes watching me the entire time. "Did you meet her at Northwestern?"

I nodded. "What about you? Still single?"

She averted her eyes and shook her head. "I met an older man. He's a partner at the accounting firm where I did my articling." Her eyes found mine again. "He takes good care of me, Cameron."

"I don't want to know what his name is," I admitted, wondering why my chest felt suddenly constricted. I was supposed to be in love with Riley. I shouldn't have cared about Hope's romantic life. I should've been happy for her. After all, it was me that disappeared. And if she were involved with someone else, I would no longer have to carry all the weight, the guilt that came with breaking our promise.

"So why did you kiss me the other night?" she asked, clearly trying to steer the conversation in a direction she wanted.

I groaned. "Let's take this back a couple of steps, shall we? Why were you *stalking* me the other night?"

She rolled her eyes. "Puh-lease, Cameron."

"It's a legitimate question," I told her, "and I really want to know what you were doing outside my townhouse in the dark. And in the rain!"

"You kissed me, mister. I didn't ask you to come running after me, or to tackle me like a fucking rapist in front of your community center." She shook her head at me, huffing. "And I swear you touched my boob, too. If you'd just let me go, *none* of this would've happened, and you'd be at home right now, making dinner for Riley and playing house."

"Is that what you wanted? For me to just notice you, then let you slip away?"

She avoided the question and allowed her attention to wander about the interesting graffiti that made this restaurant so unique in its decor.

"It's going to take another forty minutes or so for our pizza," I informed her. "We may as well talk this through, Hope."

She abruptly moved her attention back, her eyes stern and unflinching. "Then let's start with that kiss, Cameron."

"Which was inspired by your stalking," I elaborated with a slight smile.

She shook her head again. "You tell me about the kiss, and I'll tell you what I was doing outside your townhouse."

I opened my mouth to protest, but she held up one of her long fingers, and I noticed just how sexy her nails were—the dark polish, the smooth edging. I missed those fingers between mine, missed those nails digging into my back.

"I asked the question first, Cameron. So you answer me first, and I swear I'll answer you."

I took a deep breath and sat back against the graffiti-ridden booth. "The truth?" I paused, and she just kept watching me with those eyes. "I had to kiss you. It was the right thing to do."

She crossed her arms, the fresh smirk on her face suggesting that we had travelled back in time. "The 'right' thing to do, huh?" This was the *us* of seven years ago, the happy times and the tense times all rolled into one. "What does that mean, Cameron? The *right* thing to do?" She shook her head at me.

"You were there." I motion to her, gesturing and allowing myself to retreat to those memories. "You were in my arms. Your face was close, and we were one. Just like before. I kissed you because you were there again. It was you and me, and the only thing that felt right, at that specific moment, was kissing you."

Her blank stare said maybe I had gone a little too far. But it was the truth; it was how I had felt.

"So, Hope?" Now it was her turn. "Why were you creeping on me? It's been seven years, I never thought I'd see you again."

The egotistical pleasure I found in her face just moments ago seemed to deflate. She let out a long breath, and it felt like she was letting out the helium from a birthday balloon, releasing the essence and jovial mood of the party. And I knew, just watching her, that maybe some things were best left unspoken.

I reached across the table for her hands. "It's okay," I told her. "We can talk about something else. It's really not that important."

"Thank you," she said, but it lacked finality. She wanted to talk about this.

"Seven years, huh?" I was trying to change the subject. I even forced an incredulous whistle. "Wow, time fucking flies."

"It was a promise," she said, hissing a little. "You broke my heart when you left, and you broke it again when you stopped responding to my emails. And you want to know why I stood outside your townhouse in the pouring rain, Cameron?"

I held my hands up. "No, actually I don't." I forced a chuckle that sounded about as genuine as a plastic Rolex. "I'm pretty sure I said we could talk about something else." I cleared my throat. "So how do you enjoy being an accountant?"

She leaned closer on the table, and I knew where this was headed before the hurt and rage dripped from her lips. "Fuck you, Cameron. For years I wondered what was wrong with me. I wondered what I could've done to chase you off, why I wasn't good enough for you, why you chose something or someone else instead of coming back to me."

"It was nothing you did—"

She propelled forward, fueled by all those years of my neglect. Her response surprised me. "I wondered what kind of asshole you really were. What changed? How could we have gone from soul mates and being so madly in love to…to nothing? I beat myself up for years over this. Seven long fucking years." She smacked the table to hammer her point home.

"You shouldn't have, Hope, it was—" I started, but she interrupted me, and I bit down on my tongue.

"I beat myself up for ever agreeing to anything. For letting you in, for letting you go, for letting you take my heart with you wherever it was that you disappeared to. Which was here, in Chicago, this whole time."

I sighed, speechless and a little defeated. I counted to ten to see if she had more to say. She did.

"I searched for years, Cameron." Her voice was small, almost inaudible.

I grasped for the first excuse I could find. "My parents could've told you where to find me. You know that. If you really wanted to find me—"

Her eyes spit fire at me. Again. "I would never have done that."

Finally, I asked her the question I really wanted to know. "Then how did you find me, Hope?"

"LinkedIn," she said. "It brought me to Chicago. It brought me to Harris, to your office building. And from there, it wasn't hard to track you, wasn't hard to blend into the crowds that walk to the train station every night after work."

"How long did you…?" My words quieted as I pictured it. She'd been trailing me?

"Two weeks. Last Friday was the first night I followed you all the way home. And, while I stood outside your townhouse in the rain, watching you kiss that girl—who is the polar opposite of me, by the way—and make dinner, and do all of those domesticated things that I always imagined *we* would do together," she tapped her heart with her fist, "I thought I had my answer. Why you disappeared on me."

She sipped her iced tea, and as I watched her, I memorized the features I had lived so long without—the lines of her face, the creases at the corners of her eyes, the way her upper lip seemed a little smaller than her pouty lower lip, the scar underneath her jawline on the left side of her face, the mole on her neck.

She was right, though. We had promised those things to each other, those domestic things that made life regular and painful; but with Hope, those chores would've made the world come alive.

She started again, slowly, "What started out as five minutes turned into ten, then half an hour, then two hours. I didn't notice how drenched the rain had made me until you tackled me. But I had my answer, Cameron. Until you ran after me and kissed me, I had every answer I had come for, the answers to what it was that stole you from me and destroyed everything that made the past seven years without you so painful. Oddly, I was at peace."

"But I ran after you," I murmured, "instead of letting you go."

"And you kissed me." She shook her head, peeking up at me from staring down at her hands. "Everything came rushing back with that kiss. It felt so right, so perfect. Just being there…with you…in your arms…and now here we are. At a pizza joint that takes all night to make a deep-dish pie."

She wiped at the edge of her eyes, but I didn't see tears. I saw the dryness and emptiness left by shattered dreams, a broken heart, and something I could never replace—even if I picked her up in my arms right that instant and rode off into the sunset with her.

PRESENT DAY

CHAPTER 23

9:28 AM

Reaching into my pocket after we finish eating breakfast, I pull out a single piece of paper. I look up, but only briefly enough to see whether Hope's eyes have noticed the paper in my hands. They haven't; she seems distracted by the view out the window facing the train tracks, the city view. So I start reading what is written on that paper.

"I believe," I say, just loudly enough to catch her attention. "I believe you live once and that better opportunities are lost on second chances. I believe true love is about as real as Santa Claus, but 'tis the season, so let's play this game...I believe that you fall in 'love' with the person who lets you love him or her the way you want, on your terms. I believe if someone says he 'loves you more than air,' he's lying to you. I believe that love is not about forgiveness. It's about acceptance, and acceptance keeps relationships alive. I believe in the stories that are never told. I believe that if you have to fight for love, you're trying to force a square peg into a round hole. I believe that your flaws are what make you beautiful. Deal with it."

"Cameron," she sighs, but I see the glint of recognition in her eyes. "What are you doing?"

I ignore her and continue reading from the page. "I believe that two people are just that—two people. I believe that two married people are two individuals with one shared goal and one shared delusion. I believe delusions are a good thing until you start involving drugs, threesomes, and whips. Stay pure. I believe that in your heart, you have blood not love. And that blood is to the heart what ideas, not love, are to the mind. I believe that happy endings happen in real life when I fall asleep, thinking of the smiles on the faces of the children I want to have. I believe that all stories are written for me—that same story means something different for you, and that's okay. I believe in freedom for everyone; everyone has the right to hunt or to hide or both. I believe that mothers are sacred, and anyone who tells a mother what to do has self-esteem issues. I believe that true character gets revealed in actions, not in what someone says about himself. I believe that 'promise' is one word, and any one word means nothing. I believe that if you never hurt, you never find happiness; the bigger you hurt, the bigger your happiness. I believe in friendships that last a lifetime and in friends that support you even when you are dead wrong. I believe that most of the decisions you make are the wrong ones. So celebrate your victories, celebrate hard because they're rare. I believe that if you can make decisions objectively, you will never be wrong. Or hurt. Or happy. I believe that we cry for ourselves, not for others. I believe that tears are a lot like rage—you need to get that poison out of your system periodically, or it will kill you."

"Cameron, of course I remember this." She pulls at her collar and shakes her head at me, her face a little red at having heard the words she had written to me so long ago. "Are you happy now? Happy I remember? Now can we forget about it and get out of here?"

"Just let me finish," I insist, dropping my attention back to the page. "I believe that when you die, you die alone, and…" I pause because this part always killed me. "And I believe that goodbyes are forever." I fold the paper and tuck it back into my pocket. "You wanted to know if I remembered a promise from seven years ago?"

Hope stares outside again, and when she speaks after a moment that seems to stretch into an eternity, her words come out in a whisper. "Let it go."

I poke myself in the chest, my throat tight. "I remember, Hope. I fucking *live* with your fucked up beliefs every day of my life."

"Those are *my* words," she says, her voice quiet but firm as she brings her attention back to me. "I wrote them, Cameron. I wrote them when you stopped."

Her face twists with confusion. "Stopped? Stopped what? Stopped answering your crazy calls? Stopped responding to your angry emails?"

"You just *stopped.* All I knew and believed in was *us*, and then you stopped. To me, you stopped loving and knowing me. So no, I didn't believe in promises, I didn't believe in love. And yes, I wrote those words for you. So you would remember."

"How could I *ever* forget, Hope? Do you still believe that stuff you wrote? That love doesn't exist? That all we have in our hearts is blood? That you die alone and goodbyes are forever?" I force a slight chuckle. Those words crushed me and robbed me of precious sleep during midterms, and I hated Hope for that, for nailing that final nail into the coffin. We had a *promise.*

"Why did you stop?" she asked. "It wasn't the poem."

Her question has haunted me all of these years. I still don't know why I "stopped," but I do know that I enjoyed the freedom. Not right away, but after that first semester I sure did. And having that five-year promise in my back pocket helped me feel secure, too. It was my insurance policy. I figured, if nothing better came along, Hope would be waiting for me at the end of that term, and until then, I was supposed to live the life all men fantasized about.

But then I met Riley, and I sort of forgot about Hope, filed her in the back of my mind and allowed that insurance policy to expire. It became easier to think we could just go our separate ways, no hard feelings, no harm done. Because Riley would *never* have agreed to a two-day promise, let alone a five-year one that would leave my spirit crushed and my heart split in two.

Except I kept finding this poem Hope had written for me.

"Cameron, tell me why you stopped."

The restaurant staff starts moving the other tables back into place, getting ready for their regular dining hours. I smirk at her. "I think it's time for us to leave."

"Just tell me!" Her tone has a joking edge to it, but I know she wants the answer to why I disappeared. "Tell me why you stopped!"

I push my chair out and stand up, shrugging. "Maybe another time, Hope. Let's get out of here."

"Fucking goob," she curses, standing up and walking with me to the doors to the Art Institute of Chicago. "Don't think for one minute I don't know what you're doing," she adds, falling into stride next to me. "But you *will* tell me why you stopped."

CHAPTER 24

9:58 AM

I'm staring at my face in the mirror, running a finger along the smile lines and wondering how I got so old, so fast. I'm not even thirty yet, but these lines shouldn't exist. I shouldn't look at my face and feel like life has sucked the good years out of me. Not yet.

But life has sucked those good years out of me. This mess with Hope is largely to blame because sometimes, when you love someone this much, that kind of love strips you of something.

I know this. Even Riley knows this. I'm just not so sure that Hope knows this.

When another man enters the bathroom and slides into one of the stalls so quietly that it's obvious he doesn't want anyone to notice him, it's time to leave. I wash and dry my hands then climb the grand stairwell all the way to the top floor. I pause when I find Hope standing in front of a Monet painting. It's the *Arrival of the Normandy Train, Gare Saint-Lazare*, and it's perfect. Each stroke of Monet's brush makes me feel something in my chest. I don't get to think too much about what that sensation means, though.

Hope turns away from the Monet and studies me.

"Everything okay?" she asks, stepping up to me. Her heels clack and smother me with memories of all those times we had spent together when we should have been doing something else.

I nod past her at the painting, reveling in the coconut that wafts off her hair and across my nostrils like a summer breeze. "The first person you see in the painting, what do you think about?"

She considers my face for a beat before spinning around and moving back to the Monet. I edge a little closer, too, wanting to smell her perfume, taste it, memorize it because I know what today could mean for a thirty-year-old man who feels like life is almost over.

I watch her left hand rise, and she points to the largest figure in the impressionist painting. "That's the first person I see."

"He's the closest," I admit. "But what do you think when you see him?"

She takes a second or two before answering. "He's alone."

"And the next person you see?"

She motions to the second closest figure, a little to the left of the first one, the one I originally had in mind. "Alone."

I reach down for her right hand and point to the right side of the painting. "Yet these people closer to the train, we see tons of them." I bring my lips within inches of her ear. "Nobody wants to arrive at their destination only to be greeted by loneliness, do they?"

She says nothing. I trace my hand from her fingers, all the way up her arm, to her slender shoulder, then flip my hand around so the back of my fingers slide up her neck and circle around her ear.

"Cameron," she breathes, tilting her neck so subtly that

anyone else probably would not have even noticed. I see the vein that betrays all of her emotions and want to lick it, but I keep my mouth (and tongue) to myself. Not part of the plan.

"Look at me," I tell her instead, swallowing a deep gulp to regain my composure. "My fucking eyes, Hope. Tell me what you see in my eyes."

She refuses to turn around, even with the little nudge of encouragement from my hand that has fallen back down to her shoulder. Instead, Hope shakes her head.

"I believe…" I say, referring to her poem.

"Stop it, Cameron," she whispers.

So I stop. I move my attention back to the painting, my eyes catching on the smoke rising from the train's funnel. Each stroke points me to the next puff of smoke from another steam engine, the one pulling into the station. And this makes me think about something I have never considered before.

I take a step backward, reaching down to Hope's hand to lure her away from the Monet. This was the only reason I wanted to bring her here—to see *this* painting. There is a reason for that, and she knows it.

"Who's waiting for those people, the ones on that other train, Hope?" I ask. There is nobody waiting on that platform.

Abruptly, she spins around and walks past me, deeper into the museum. "I'm done here, Cameron."

three years ago

CHAPTER 25

I woke Saturday morning to the softness of lips kissing my eyelids. And she whispered, "Wake up, sunflower." More kisses, and then, "It's Saturday." And then reality slowly set in.

The voice didn't belong to Hope, though; it belonged to Riley. Only Hope called me sunflower. But she wasn't the first to kiss my eyelids as a way to wake me up, and she knew that.

Snapping awake, I scooted away from her kind and gentle lips, startling her. She stepped out of bed, wearing nothing but her white slip and flowing blonde hair.

"Cam, what's wrong?" She wasn't exactly glaring at me, but the look on her face suggested she was not impressed. At all.

Fuck. I rubbed the sleep out of my eyes and rolled onto my side. I patted the empty space in bed, inviting her back.

"How late were you out last night?" she asked.

"I don't know," I answered, but I knew. Of course I knew. "Come lay with me."

Riley considered it, but not for long. She shook her head. "I'm going to have a shower. I have to go back into the city. I forgot those Bulls tickets at the office." She stripped out of her slip, her smallish, perky breasts flopping out. I loved her nipples, so I watched her. She knew it, too, because she stopped at the foot of the bed, full frontal, and asked, "Want to come?"

I smiled but shook my head. "Rain check, I'm sorry. I have a bit of work to finish up this morning."

"Cam, I thought that was why you were working so late all week?" she complained. "So we could have our weekend to ourselves."

Shit. "I know. It's not much, though. Just a few reports I need to pretty up."

"And I didn't mean come with me into the city. I meant why don't you come with me in the shower?" She winked, biting on her lower lip.

I very deliberately admired her entire body, my eyes crawling up and down, first getting lost in that galaxy of freckles on her upper chest, then rolling over the small bump of her belly that you couldn't see underneath any clothing, but was absolutely perfect. Still, I could think of nothing else but Hope, which wasn't cool at all. When my stare reached the small patch of soft pubic hair, I abruptly moved my attention back to her face, feeling guilty. Like I was cheating on Hope with my soon-to-be bride.

I sat up in bed. "I'm going to get started on my work bullshit, so we can have the rest of the day together."

The deflated look on her face told me she knew. Maybe not about last night's laughing and flirting and how Hope and I had latched onto each other for a breath longer than we should have when we said goodbye. But she recognized that I was distracted.

"Okay." She started walking away, then stopped at the

bedroom door to glance back at me. "Everything okay, Cam? You've been acting all strange these past couple of weeks."

I could've corrected her. Technically, it had only been since last Friday, eight days ago. Instead, I gave her a shrug. "It's nothing, really."

"Bullshit." She shook her head.

"Work's busy, and if anything," I said, taking a deep breath, "it's probably just pre-wedding jitters."

Riley didn't like that response. She strolled back into the bedroom, her hands on her hips, her scowl beating down on me like the desert sun. It was blinding all right. "Jitters, huh?"

I chuckled, pulling the blankets over my lap like they could protect me. "I think it's all pretty standard, Riley." I swallowed hard, nodding past her at the door. "Go have your shower…we're wasting time with this."

She kept her eyes on me a little longer than she should have, then finally turned and walked away. I watched her ass as she left, wondering what had gone so wrong, so quickly.

Fuck, Hope.

I massaged my face and waited to hear the shower spray before finally jumping out of bed and hurrying to the other bedroom to set up my work laptop at the desk. While the computer booted up, I stared out the window at the townhouse across from us, remembering that night.

Fuck, Hope.

I returned my attention to the computer and found an email.

Well, I found half a dozen, but there was one in particular that stopped my heart.

Fuck, Hope.

I saw that there was an attachment to that email, so I opened the message and stared at the paperclip icon. I was hoping for a picture, preferably a nude or semi-nude one, but when I looked a little closer, I read the file extension and saw that it was just a fucking document. I cursed, the words silent on my mouth when—

"Cam, I'm heading out."

I swung around in my chair like she had just caught me watching porn and masturbating. I wiped my clammy palms along my legs because in so many ways, this thing with Hope was a million times worse than online adult movies. "Okay. Yeah. Sure."

From her position in the doorway, Riley tilted her head, scrutinizing me. "You've been weird all morning. Maybe you should get some more sleep, huh?"

I nodded, ready to agree with almost anything just to get her out of the house so I could open that non-visual attachment and see what it was all about.

"Okay, why don't we meet at the Starbucks in my building at noon?" She strolled into the room, but I didn't want her to see the message so I met her halfway, letting her fall into my arms to keep her from seeing what was on the computer screen.

"Sounds great. Noon." I kissed the top of her head, my hand on her shoulder like she might be a cousin, and Riley didn't seem to like that.

Twirling out of my grip, she reminded me about meeting her at noon, then she was gone. I walked to the window and watched her hurry out of the townhouse and rush down the laneway. Once I couldn't see her anymore, I returned to the computer and opened the attachment.

It was a fucking novel. Literally, a novel of some one hundred and eighteen pages, consisting of nothing but words. I scrolled forward through the pages to see if there were pictures to help lighten the load, but there weren't.

"This is a joke. It has to be." I brushed my hand through my hair, wondering what the whole point of this was. I clicked back to the main message screen and found her original note.

Cameron,

I'm sorry for coming back into your life so close to your wedding day. Ultimately, all I wanted out of this was to see you again, to see that you're happy. And you are. Or were. And I'm afraid I've complicated that. But before I fly back home, here's what I've been working on these last few years. It's called *Our Story*, and you've somehow inspired every single word. I didn't write it, but I'd love it if you could read it. As much as it's my story, it's not mine at all.

Enjoy it, and good luck next month with Riley. You two make a beautiful couple, so congratulations.

Hope

I read her message over and over again, at least half a dozen times as my stomach dropped, and a deep, piercing heat rose into the base of my skull. I didn't want to read a fucking novel.

I checked my watch. I had a couple of hours before I had to leave to meet up with Riley. I didn't have all fucking morning, so I skipped forward several chapters and started there.

OUR StORy OLIVIA

Waking up next to Oliver on the Monday that my flight left for home, I remember thinking that nothing had ever felt worse than what I felt at that moment. We had fallen asleep holding each other. But this morning I found him with his back to me, his black T-shirt rising out from the mess of white sheets that had enveloped us a few hours earlier.

Reaching out, I pulled the sheets onto his shoulder, covering him. It wasn't so much that I feared he would get cold, but…I hated that he had rolled away from me, that I had slept with the false belief that he'd been holding me in his arms this entire time.

With Oliver, everything changed from the moment my name dripped off his tongue. Even if I didn't exactly believe in soul mates, I believed in…well, us.

I edged closer to him on the bed and wrapped my arms around him from behind, just as he had done to me the night before. And then I curled my legs around his and buried my face into the back of his neck, breathing in all of him. It felt so perfect, lying here with him. Yes, lying—as much on the bed as to each other, to the people in our lives.

"Did we do anything last night?" he asked, his voice coarse first thing in the morning. "My arm fell asleep under your neck." He rolled over, and the dark circles under his eyes told me he hadn't slept well.

I nodded, smiling. "Yes."

He leaned a touch closer. "I need to kiss you."

With Oliver, I fought for love because he made me believe in something I never knew to be missing from my life. Until now.

Following my trip to Chicago, I returned to my real life in Vegas, which meant selling mortgages and other financial services to everyday folks who wanted bigger and better than they could afford. That first day back was difficult, but it was a Tuesday and quiet. While I waited at my desk for a lender to get back to me on a "tight" application, I swung my chair around and stared out my window at one of the most notorious skylines in the country. Even as a local, I thought it looked fake. Just like I imagined it would appear to people who had never visited Vegas and only ever saw it on movie or television screens.

"Oliver Weaver," I whispered to myself, "what have you done to me?"

From my office, I could also watch the airlines come and go every ten minutes or so. Each time I noticed an airplane, I wondered—okay, I *prayed*—that Oliver would be aboard, that he would come for me and take me away. Life without him was a silent film.

When my phone chirped, I snatched it up right away. "Olivia Warren," I nearly shouted, my heart beating hard inside my chest. I never acted like a schoolgirl when my phone rang. But when I heard his voice, I knew why.

This relationship with Oliver, whatever it meant, was different than anything I had ever experienced before. I just didn't know it yet.

A couple of months had passed since my trip to Chicago, and I was preparing dinner at the stove, working on a special scallops and rice recipe when that hard heartbeat returned to me. I stepped away from my work, sat down at the table, and tried to regain control.

It was getting dark outside, and the air had cooled. Maybe the change in temperature was to blame. Really, I didn't know what this heartbeat thing meant, but I wondered if it could also have something to do with an earlier conversation I had with Oliver. We spoke for nearly an hour earlier today, when my boss was at a client's house to sign documents.

"You okay?" my husband asked from the living room. "I'm fucking starving here." Yes, he was a dickhead, but he had plans to go out with the boys tonight, which meant I would have the place to myself.

I nodded without looking at him. "I'm fine."

Returning to the stove, I checked on the scallops, then pulled the rice off the stove. I slopped a couple of servings onto our plates. Instead of sitting at the table, I told him that I needed some fresh air. He said nothing. He may not have even heard me, like a child who needs countless reminders to get their shoes on for school.

I slipped outside to our front porch, which wrapped around our house, and I stepped up to the railing. The darkness made it hard to see—not that deep-black dark of a moonless sky at two in the morning, but that confusing, hazy dark right before the sun disappears for good.

An airplane roared overhead, and I caught myself tracing its path with my eyes, watching it and wondering where it was headed. Chicago? And then it started again, that wild and crazy heartbeat that made me weak and worried at the same time. *Oh, Oliver, where are you?*

"I'm here," he said, seemingly stepping out of another dimension. He wore straight-leg jeans and a white button-down shirt with brown leather shoes. They were gorgeous shoes, but I took in all of him.

I glanced back toward the front door, then the large living room window that allowed me to see my husband at the table, still eating.

"I just want to smell your hair," he said, stepping carefully into the neglected garden that bordered our porch.

"What are you doing here?" I whispered. "My husband will kick your ass if he finds you here."

Oliver seemed surprised. "He knows about me?"

"No, but if he finds you, he will!" I chuckled, not because he said anything funny, but because I was so excited to see him here that I couldn't keep the happy off my face. "Give me half an hour," I told him. "Tim's going out tonight, but I'll meet you in town."

I heard my husband shouting something inside.

"I'll meet you in half an hour," I whispered again, whipping my head around to make sure he wasn't coming for me, and then turned back to Oliver. "Half an hour, okay?"

"Where?" he asked me, the grin stretching from one side of his face to the next.

Shrugging, I said his hotel.

He smiled. "I'm at the Hard Rock."

I entered the house to my husband's bitching and moaning about his game shirt being dirty, and the rest of it sort of blurred into the bullshit of marital bliss. For once, I didn't fall into the argument trap. I quietly slipped upstairs while he yelled at the dishwasher, slamming his plate and fork into the right slots, then going on about how much of a moron I could be, or something like that. In the bedroom, I grinned at my isolation, at the lump in the middle of our mattress that spoke quite clearly as to just how "close" Tim and I had become over the past ten years.

I crashed onto that same lumpy mattress, grabbed a book, and pretended that I could see the words through the film of Oliver-fog on my eyes.

We had a quiet corner table at Nobu in the Hard Rock Casino building. It wasn't busy at all. Then again, a lot of people were probably gambling or watching the game, like Tim. The quiet ambiance allowed me time to really watch Oliver, drink him in.

"You're here," I said while he continued talking about his "surprise" trip to Vegas for a conference a senior partner couldn't make on account of some personal issues. I really didn't care about the circumstances. We'd spoken earlier today when he was at the office, and he was there, in Chicago, but now he was here, in Vegas, in front of me. I took his hand and squeezed it. "You're here and I missed you and now I'm breathing again." I closed my eyes and took a deep breath as if inhaling him, all of him.

"Yes, I'm here, Olivia." He chuckled, lifting my hand to his lips and kissing each of my fingers. He had always done that, it was something that belonged exclusively to Oliver, something we didn't share with our spouses—it was ours. "Why is this so weird all of a sudden?"

I opened my eyes and told him that I missed him. "I've dreamed about you a million times."

He chuckled again, and his smile allowed me to imagine lifetimes spent with him.

"Today, Oliver. I'm talking about today only. I dream about you more and more every moment we spend apart. But now you're here. And you're mine for how long?"

His forehead rippled with the inevitability of our limited time together. "I've got the conference on Sunday, and I'm flying out Monday morning," he said, almost apologetically.

Our sushi arrived. Oliver wore his wedding ring, and I still wore mine—I could have removed it after my husband left with "the boys," cursing the whole time that he had to wear a dirty Buccs jersey, which wasn't dirty. I hadn't removed anything except my clothes, replacing the pantsuit with a pair of jeans and a blouse, so Oliver and I looked like a couple.

What probably indicated to others that we were not spouses to one another was the happiness at our table.

"Try this," Oliver said, pinching a spicy tuna roll and feeding it to me.

I found a dragon roll on my plate and did the same for him, all the while wondering what married couple fed one another like we did.

"This is us, isn't it?" Oliver asked, almost chuckling at the sweetness of our motions.

I agreed with him, but I still doubted that we would always be like this, that this utopic happiness would endure years and years of togetherness.

We laughed and flirted and fed each other like two college kids who needed to get laid. Once we finished, Oliver asked me if I wanted to come upstairs. "It's a suite because that's what our firm's partners get when they travel. Which means the minibar is covered. As well as room service for dessert." He sounded a little nervous, but then slid his arm around my waist and pinched my side playfully to cover it up. "And you can afford dessert."

"Shut up!" I laugh, swatting his hands away from my sides—could always lose a few pounds, tighten up my abs. "You know exactly why I haven't been eating."

I accompanied him to his room, and just like he promised, he had a nice big suite. As soon as we entered, we stood motionless on the other side of the door and just stared at each other. I was still breathing him in, memorizing every possible detail. But once that door closed, I jumped into his arms, wrapping my legs around his waist and holding him with such ferocity, I worried I might hurt him.

We kissed like we had done this kissing business a million times before. The familiarity of our lips pressed together felt like home. I loved this man wholly and completely, every inch of him. And it was the kind of love that would never end, never go away, no matter how I hard I would try over the years ahead of us.

The months following Oliver's trip to Vegas passed with a swift permanence that I could only compare to head-butting an oncoming freight train. There was pain, yes. But it felt like months before I could appreciate it, before I finally awoke from the coma of the sudden impact. That painful change began the moment I stepped through the door late Sunday afternoon, after spending Friday and Saturday night with Oliver at the Hard Rock.

My husband was drunk—typical Sunday afternoon

bullshit—with the Raiders game playing on the television in the background. When he heard the front door opening, he called me something nasty. Still dreamy from my time with Oliver, I stepped deeper into the house, noticing the kitchen sink, dishes all piled up. An open pizza box with the crust still inside and flies crawling around told me Saturday night had been a lonely one for him as well.

I stopped at the edge of the living room, disgusted by the crumbs on the floor next to the sofa where he watched the game with his back to me. Yet I was the one with the nasty nickname. Right.

"Where were you?" he demanded.

"You're a slob, Tim. This place is fucking gross."

"It'll be clean tonight. Now where the fuck have you been sleeping, you fucking whore?"

I stood there, watching him. I didn't have to think too long about my next statement. Like driving in a blizzard or a sandstorm, I saw only as far as the few feet in front of me, not the miles between here and my ultimate destination.

At last, my husband turned around, his eyes red and puffy, his beard unshaven. I swore his teeth had gone yellow, and I shuddered at the prospect of just how foul his breath might be. Despite his obvious rage, I stepped forward.

"I'm not asking again, bitch," he said. "Where the fuck have you—"

"Done. I'm done with your bullshit, Tim." I glanced back at the sink and gave it an elaborate wave—it was a scene that repeated itself at least a couple dozen weekends every year, a reminder of his laziness and how he cared about nothing and no one but himself. "You're fucked without me; we both know it."

He laughed, a crazy laugh that reminded me of what made me fall in love with him in the first place—that craziness, seemingly untamable, so new and foreign to me. But it also reminded me of everything I now hated about him.

Standing on unsteady feet, he approached me.

I wasn't scared of him, not anymore. I was tired. "You're fucked without me," I repeated, and I tasted the venom on my words. I decided at that moment that no man would ever walk all over me ever again. Starting right now.

My husband stopped and swayed, but, by some miracle, he kept his balance. He was close enough to hit me, but far enough away that if he swung and I stepped backward, he would fall flat on his face.

"I'm leaving you," I told him, because Oliver made me believe in the impossibility of love being all that I'd ever need. The finality of my promise turned his eyes a bloodshot red.

His face tightened, possibly with confusion, but judging by the way his brows slanted inwardly toward the bridge of his nose, there was a dare in there, too. "You've never been alone," he hissed, but there was the hint of something else in there, too. "Either you're fucking someone else, or you're just pissed about the mess."

I shook my head, a slow and deliberate motion that allowed me to keep my eyes glued to his as his pupils flickered from side to side. The weekend with Oliver had given me more strength than I had ever thought possible. "I'm done. Either you let me pack my things and walk out of here, or I walk out without them, and you're stuck going through them on your own. Either way, I don't care. I'm leaving. I'm done with you."

He wiped his wrist across his lips, unblinking. "Nobody will take you. You're fucking crazy. And you suck in bed."

I laughed at him. If only he had felt, tasted, and lived what I had these past two nights. Not just the muscular contractions of orgasm, but the true, inseparable sensation of being loved by someone. It wasn't about sucking in bed, but it was definitely *all about* being crazy.

A forced half-smile rose on his lips, but I didn't fall for it; those lips camouflaged the underlying fury. "You want your stuff?" he asked me. "Before you get the fuck out of my face, you dirty cunt?"

I shrugged my shoulder, noticing the tension in my upper-back had climbed into my neck. "Your choice. I don't care."

My husband had a gift. He could move swiftly. But with so much alcohol in his veins, his aim was all wrong. He missed my face entirely and collapsed. I moved aside so he couldn't grab my ankles and pull me down with him.

"You're pathetic," I spat, leaning forward so I could get as close to his face as I safely dared. "And you don't deserve me. You don't deserve anyone or anything. You treat me like shit. And you think anyone will want to lay next to your drunk, fat ass?" I shook my head, chuckling again. "You have nothing to offer. Nothing."

"Get out," he whispered to the floor, but I knew his words were for me.

I leaned in a little closer to this slob on the floor, his gut visible between the waist of his elastic band and the stained shirt. "Not even to yourself."

"Get out!" he screamed, flailing because he was just too washed up to do anything else.

And so I left. With nothing except my bank card and a credit card that I had obtained in college.

The Barney's coffee house in Winnetka had bistro tables out front that faced the main street and a private patio out back that faced a quiet parking lot. Usually only the loners sat out back, seeking peace and quiet to read or write, or even meditate with their capps or lattes. Since the neighboring buildings cast long shadows and kept the sun out, few extroverts or couples opted for that back patio. Nobody saw you out there, not like the bistro tables out front.

I sat out back, just like Oliver had asked. For one, he couldn't risk his wife or kids walking by and seeing us out front, and since Barney's brewed Oliver's favorite coffee beans, if he was out too long, chances were quite high that his wife might come looking for him inside as well.

But never out back.

Out back seemed reserved for those loners.

Or lovers.

I waited for the 349 train to arrive and when I heard its bell at 6:01 (*early, yay!*), I retreated inside and ordered a non-fat cappuccino before reclaiming my table out back in the shade. The train station was close, less than a ten-minute walk. So I waited fifteen minutes, then decided to drink the cappuccino rather than waste it.

I waited for the 351 train to arrive, and when I heard its bell eighteen minutes later (*late, boo!*), I ordered another non-fat cappuccino and reclaimed the same table out back. This time, I waited twenty minutes before drinking my second cappuccino.

It was ten minutes after the 359 train arrived at 7:19 PM that I noticed the silhouette standing in the doorway to this back patio. I looked up from my lonely seat, my mind buzzing and half-insane. I had been crying, which meant the baristas or clerks, or whatever the fuck they were called, only asked once if I was okay.

Oliver bowed his head before pushing the door open and walking to my table, *our* table. He didn't sit down, and I didn't look up. Instead, I looked into my lap and thought of happy things—my latest book sales, the quarterly royalty check that would help me move to Chicago to be with the man I loved.

"I'm sorry," he whispered, standing there above me. Although I didn't see whatever torture occupied his face, I heard the crack in his voice, and it wasn't the kind that would ever heal. It was the kind that broke me as well, the kind my best friend, Jannie, had warned me about when I first told her about Oliver.

No matter how happy those earlier thoughts, I noticed a tear drop from my face and absorb into the thigh of my jeans. At first, it was just one, then two, and then many, and my shoulders racked back and forth. It was repulsive, it lacked grace, and when I finally found a way to bury the devastating heartbreak of our reality, I looked up from my soaking legs and saw that he was gone.

Oliver had walked away without saying goodbye.

That day, all those years ago, the air had been sucked out of my lungs, and I had to learn how to live all over again—how to eat and breathe, smile and observe—just *see* the world around me. Something that had previously been so simple and mundane had taken on an ugly hue without Oliver in my life.

Oliver was the freight train.

PRESENT DAY

CHAPTER 26

10:25 AM

When we leave the Art Institute, Hope hurries ahead of me by a few paces like she might be pissed, angry about something. I catch up to her as she hurries across Monroe and steers toward the lake. I call out a pleading "hey," but she keeps going, her heels clacking on the sidewalk. As I fall into step next to her, I slide my hand across her lower back, but she rolls away and takes an open-handed swing at me. I duck away, feeling the smack of air waft past my face. I can't help but chuckle.

"What am I doing, Cameron?" She grabs her hair, forces her eyes closed, and shakes her head. "What are *we* doing? This is so wrong."

I reach for her hands, but she steps back.

"No, Cameron. I'm going." She continues toward the lake again, so I join her.

"Let's just go to the park. We can sit by the waterfall or the big, reflective kidney bean, or whatever the fuck it is."

"Why?"

I stay quiet until we reach the corner of Monroe and

Columbus, where the concrete stairs lead back into the park. Once she stops, Hope crosses her arms and stares across the street.

"Hope," I beg, giving her a mild pout, just enough to show her I care, but not too much to look like a whiny little bitch. "It's all good; it's a fucking gorgeous day. It should be illegal to work on days like this." Because she hasn't taken another swing at me, or continued walking, I carry on with my plea. "Give me until lunch. We'll meet Gordo and have a light meal, but until then, why don't we…" I nod up the stairs. "Have you seen Millennium Park?"

She stares off in the other direction, then shakes her head. "Just tell me why. You're married, and I'm in love with Matt. This? Our 'sick day' together? It's sweet and everything, but it's not changing anything."

"Okay," I agree, stepping closer to her. "Nothing changes. But at least I have this day with you. Please. Why can't you just give me that, this last day before you move and I walk away, just like I promised?"

She swivels on her heels and starts climbing the concrete stairs. I know that the Monet might have been a little too much for her because in *Our Story* it seemed to be a lot for Olivia, too.

While standing at the mirrored jelly bean thing that seems to fascinate all sorts of people—I still don't understand this art piece, and I wonder if half of the others in this crowd are trying to figure it out just like I am—Hope glances over at me and gives me a half-shrug. Her simple act reminds me of some of the times we spent together in our lost past. It means she has something on her mind.

"What is it?" I ask, hoping to get her talking again, anxious for her to just loosen up and live a little.

She stares at the bean.

"Hope," I say, stepping close enough to her that I can actually taste the soft perfume that wafts off her clothes with the wind. Vanilla, the bean not the ice cream. "I highly doubt you're contemplating this disturbing piece of art. And you forget I know you better than that. You can't just give me that half-shrug thing and expect me to let it go. I never have before, so why would I start now?"

She walks away, and I follow a couple of steps behind, still a little gun shy after her meltdown a few minutes ago, but also a little worried that my threat of not letting go might have crossed a few lines. As I trail her toward the waterfall sounds coming from the Crown Fountain, I dig into my pocket for my phone and notice the reel of missed messages and calls. I count half a dozen voicemail alerts from Newman, which seems about as important to me as missing a call from Riley's brother—insta-delete. But the others concern me. Eight texts from Raj, four from Gordon.

Raj: Newman says you did it. You called in sick. I hope you realize this might cost you your job if you're not careful, Cam. I've got your back, but he knows you're not sick.

Raj: Might want to forge a doctor's note…and let your doctor know about it because Newman's on a rampage. He's got the biggest hard-on for you right now.

Raj: That crazy motherfuck just left my office with your employee file and a paper copy of your absences. You owe me, fucktart.

I chuckle at his use of the word *fucktart*, mostly because I hear his accent in the text. I skip through to his last message, the mist from the fountain reaching us as we turn the corner and step through the trees.

Raj: Heads up today, Cam! Newman just left the office, and I think he's coming for you.

"Fuck," I whisper under my breath as we step onto the dark concrete with the two fountain structures spewing water.

Hope glances back before veering off toward the benches. I

follow her, sitting next to her while my eyes scan the traffic on Michigan, the faces in the crowd.

"Cameron, I see what you're doing. Or what you're trying to do. But I won't be staying behind next week." She stares into her lap and picks at her fingers. "I'm sorry, but my life is with Matt now. It's where I belong."

I let out a long breath, still deliberating the herd of tourists here at the fountain and out there on the street. Even with Newman clearly determined to catch me playing hooky today so he can fire me once and for all, I never considered aborting my plans for today, regardless of what Hope said or threatened or promised. All it takes is a look, a glance even. Hope's heart has not changed or aged; to my eyes, everything about her remains as perfect and flawless as ever.

When her big eyes find mine, I see that something is lacking, despite her words.

"Conviction," I say, mostly to myself because *that*, I am certain, is what's missing.

"Pardon me?"

Realizing a little too late that I spoke the word aloud, I shake my head and tell her about Raj's email. "You were right, my boss doesn't like me very much. He thinks what I do with my analysis and financial psychology is just bullshit. Yes, I'm paid well, and yes, our executive team has a soft spot for me. But Newman…" I shake my head. "He wants me gone so he can get back to his archaic way of designing products and programs."

"He's threatened," Hope tells me.

"What about you, Hope?" I ask, happy with myself that she has taken the "he feels threatened" route. "Is accounting really as rewarding as you thought it would be?"

She tells me a little about her work and one of the relationships she has built with a client, whose bookkeeper was stealing cash. "It's the toughest thing to tell someone. The look in their faces when you let them know that a trusted employee and, in a lot of these cases, a good *friend* is taking financial advantage of them because of their position…" She shakes her head.

"I bet that's the worst part of your job." For all I know, replacing the printer tape on her calculator could be the worst, but I try to empathize with her anyway.

"What else are we doing today, Cameron?" she asks, making a point of staring straight ahead to let me know our conversation about our careers has ended.

"We're telling Matt you don't love him anymore," I reveal to her with so much confidence, there's enough for both of us.

She allows a laugh, a good and healthy one. "We've already talked about this."

"Two months ago—"

"Was a mistake, and you know it." She puts some distance between us without ever moving away from me—her words do a good enough job that she doesn't even have to move an inch. "Have you told Riley?"

"Have you told Matt?" I counter, not seeing the relevance in her question.

And then we fall into a respectful silence.

"Riley left," I tell her at last. "She just left."

Hope mumbles an empty, "I'm sorry."

"She knows it's you, knows that all of this time has been a waste for her. Because of you, Hope."

Sighing, she rolls her eyes. "All right, goob, I get it. Homewrecker extraordinaire here. I said I'm sorry."

"It's not your fault, though," I assure her, and start reaching for her arm but think better of it because I know how sensitive she can get when I touch her. "My heart, it's all yours, Hope. You own my thoughts, my focus…you own me. Since running into you again…" I shake my head, closing my eyes. Deep breath. Here goes. "You want to know what this is all about? If you're not going to stay behind, then it's about closure. It's about allowing myself to know, one hundred percent, that I tried. That I fought." I turn my attention to her. "That I tried to fit a round peg into a square hole."

She chuckles and corrects me, "I actually wrote *square* peg into a *round* hole."

"So you really do remember!"

"Cameron…" She shakes her head.

"But you remember, and your flaws are your perfection. Nobody knows them or loves them like I do, Hope." I slide my fingers lightly across her knee, aware of the scar there. Her eyes flutter at my touch. "You know that just as well as I do."

She closes herself up to me again, facing the other direction. If she decides to place her hands over her ears and shout *La la la la,* I wouldn't be surprised.

"What about kids, Hope? Why haven't you gotten pregnant yet?"

It takes her a moment to respond, and even then her voice comes out as a sigh, weak. "We're not married."

"And when will that happen?" When she doesn't offer a response, I tell her, "It won't. You've been with this guy too long, and you said it yourself, there's no true purpose in getting married."

"Maybe I've changed, Cameron. Maybe the girl you loved in high school, who shared all of those picket-fence dreams with you, maybe she doesn't exist anymore."

"Sure she does. I'm looking at her right now."

"Is that what you think?" she says, her voice breaking a little. But the broken expression on her face tells me I'm right.

"It's what I *know*, Hope." I try to touch her again, but she pulls back.

"Don't touch me," she warns.

"You're perfect."

"Perfection doesn't exist," she tells me with her stern accountant tone.

"It exists every time I look at you, every time I hear your voice, and feel you move underneath me. Or on top of me."

"Cameron, you need to stop." She licks her lips and shakes her head, but I keep my stare on her, digging into her.

"The fact is, when I look into your eyes, and you allow me to see your heart? That's perfection, Hope. So don't preach to me that it doesn't exist, because I'm looking at it."

"It's not perfection." She sounds convinced. Or blind.

I move my hand toward hers, but she scowls a final warning.

"Hope, you deserve everything you've ever wanted." I mean it, too, like every single word I have ever said to her. "You deserve that fairy tale ending, that happily ever after, that kiss on your forehead as you take your final breath."

Something shifts in those eyes of hers.

"You deserve exactly what we had," I say, clarifying myself to her. "Because until you're back in my arms like you were three years ago, two months ago…until that happens? You might spend your whole life with Matt, but you'll be looking for it—for *me*—every time you open your eyes. Trust me, I was there. And I think I was pretty fucking good at it in college, Hope. But I also know that you don't deserve a life of always looking for something you once had but let go."

We engage in something of a staring contest, and I watch the edge of her mouth curl into a disbelieving grin. "Is that what I'm looking at right now, Cameron?"

I nod my agreement.

"Then where were you all this time? What happened three years ago? Or before that?" Another sigh. "Why did you stop? Because after all of this time, you still haven't answered me."

I hear a horn before I can even contemplate the response I will give her. Looking up, I see Gordon's Tesla. He honks again from the street, his arm waving out the open driver's side window.

"Time to go," I tell her, grabbing her wrist because I really don't want Gordon to witness me getting beaten up by Hope if I touch her hand. "Earlier than he's ever been in his life, but that's probably what happens to stay-at-home fathers whose only adult interaction is obtained on private jets and weekends in exotic, expensive destinations."

Hope chuckles. "I've missed Gordon."

"No," I correct her, picking up the pace because I swear I saw Newman's unique body shape entering a Starbucks across the street. "You just think you have. He's the same idiot who desperately needs medication. Might even be worse than before, too." And just like that, our chat from two minutes ago evaporates.

Once we reach the Tesla, I open the front door for Hope, then peek inside once she's seated.

"Are you going to let me drive?" I ask Gordo.

Gordo indicates the backseat with a nod. "Jeffrey has a racing game on his Xbox back there. You can drive that Bentley you keep bitching about." And then he gives Hope his top-floor executive smile. "Nice seeing you again, Hope."

Groaning internally at his childishness, I slip into the backseat and tell him that Newman is looking for me.

"I know," Gordon answers. "That's why I came early." And then, as he merges back into traffic, he says, "We need to have a little chat. All three of us."

tHREE YEARS aGO

CHAPTER 27

Nobody loved Mondays at Harris, but the entire office was suffering from some form of "group comatose" that particular morning. As I walked through the corridors, still numb and confused from Hope's story and the weekend I had spent with Riley, I prayed the reports and demands in my office could distract me from this moment known as my life. Nodding and grinning at the few analysts and administrators who caught my attention, I wondered where Hope was, right at that instant. I wondered if she missed me already, if she was thinking about me half as much as I had been thinking about her since our Friday night dinner.

"Hey, Cam," Gordon said, falling into stride next to me. It surprised me to find him this deep into Cubeville, let alone the fact that he had spoken two words, two more than anyone else had uttered so far this morning. "We need to have a chat before you head backstage."

We called the management offices "backstage" because they were hidden behind an extra level of security and surveillance.

"It's coming down," he whispered into my ear, so quietly that nobody else would hear.

His words stopped me. "Already?"

"Yeah." He looked around at the Monday morning stillness like it had trapped us. Realistically, we were minutes from being set free. He nodded at one of the smaller meeting rooms in the middle of the sprawling workspace. "Let's chat."

I followed him into the meeting room and placed my laptop bag on the table. Neither of us sat down, but he kept his eyes on me and said it was over.

"They're giving all of us packages and asking us to sign on the dotted line, walk away, and never look back."

"Even you?"

"*Especially* me," he admitted, placing his hands on his hips and shaking his head like he didn't see this coming. "I get to tell the entire group before someone from New York rides up those same elevators in half an hour to shake my hand in front of everyone else and announce that they're going to transfer the management of this group to the head office."

"Why?"

He shrugged. "We've done our duty, and you know how the general public feels about us banks and bankers. We're too fat. We were bailed out with *their* money in '08. Don't you know that it's because of you and me, Cam, that the American economy hiccupped a few years ago?" he asked with a sarcastic bitterness to his tone. "Nothing to do with the war or some shitty fiscal policy that backfired."

"But we survived," I said, realizing this was exactly what Gordo wanted to hear from me. "Harris repaid those government loans more than three years ago."

He shook his head. "Doesn't matter. Who cares if the economy is growing, or that people are getting back to work and spending more than ever. Doesn't matter that you and I might never find jobs again, or that we don't have pensions like those fine folks at Ford, GM, and Chrysler," he ranted and started to pace. "None of it matters because we work for a fucking bank. And because of that, because of whatever optics need to be given to the US government, you and I are going to walk out of here with a bit of money. Will it be enough to feed a family for the rest of our lives? Hell no. Would it compare to a government pension? Not even close."

Grinning, I shook my head. Seemed Gordo was a little more worried about all of this than I was. He was the VP after all, not a senior manager. Tougher for someone of his stature to bounce back. I tried to lighten the mood. "You're not a Democrat anymore, huh?"

"Listen, Cam. I need you to go to your office now. There's a banker's box on your desk. Use it to pack your shit, then come down to my office to sign the paperwork. You have five minutes before security comes to get you." With that, he opened the meeting room door. But when I started to leave, he stopped me and nodded at my laptop bag. "Leave the computer with me."

I hurried to the nice office that I had considered my home for the past few years, where I had (almost) single-handedly doubled Harris's credit card revenues and cross-selling efforts through the careful execution of my consumer behaviorism theories. This twelve-by-twelve office, with a window overseeing Chicago's Loop, had been witness to all sorts of genius.

The timing sucked.

I allowed a deflated sigh to slip past my lips. With the three personal items—one of them being the lunch Riley had prepared for me—packed loosely in that single box, I dropped into my chair and propped my feet up on the desk. Shaking my head, I contemplated what would happen next. I worried that my severance would not be enough to carry me through to my next job. I wondered how the wedding would happen in a month's time, how I could take Riley away on the honeymoon we had booked on our credit cards.

And then it hit me: was this all just one sign after another?

Wiping my hands down my face, I heard a soft knock at the door. I glanced over at Raj, our Sr. Manager of Human Resources. His face looked whiter than mine. On any regular day, that was entirely impossible.

"You will be fine, Cam," he promised. I believed him, too, his words providing a tremendous sense of security, more than any severance package could.

A security guard stepped up behind him. "Say your goodbyes, Raj, you can set up a dinner date another time."

Raj forced a half-smile, but kept his eyes glued to me. "I will definitely have plenty of time soon." With a wink, he promised to keep in touch.

I nodded goodbye, briefly remembering Hope's words—*I believe that goodbyes are forever*—then returned to my melodramatic pity party. The complications of dealing with a fifty thousand dollar wedding with no income frightened me a little. Probably not as much as the coincidence of Hope's sudden reappearance in my life, though. Or the story, *Our Story*, she had emailed me a couple of days ago.

Kissing the insides of my fingertips, I smacked the computer screen, grabbed my banker's box, and walked away from the most productive and rewarding time of my life.

CHAPTER 28

With a Starbucks cappuccino to keep me company, I returned to the Harris building and waited in the lobby by the big waterfall. The security guards knew me by now and offered their nods of consolation.

Fuck you. I have a wedding in a few weeks and a promise haunting me from my youth. The last thing I need is the struggle of unemployment.

I sensed Riley before I saw or heard her.

"Cam, what's going on?" she asked.

I turned around and found her hurrying across the granite lobby floor, her forehead glistening with perspiration. She had tears in her eyes. Once she was close enough, she pulled me into a tight hug.

"I'm so sorry," she cried. Like I had lost my best friend, like the crashing of the waterfall behind us was the banging of a funeral drum, like I even cared about losing my job as much as I cared about losing Hope.

I held her at an arm's length and admitted to myself that, as much as I probably didn't deserve Hope, I sure as hell didn't deserve Riley. In her white blouse, unbuttoned to show a bit of cleavage and in desperate need of an iron, she looked frazzled. Scared. Yesterday we spent the afternoon at the United Center, decent seats at the Bulls game—they beat the Heat by four, but it still felt like a painful victory—followed up by a nice dinner on the West end. We laughed like we used to. And when we got home, I fucked her so hard… but the last thing on my mind was Hope, or her little novel.

I didn't deserve this beautiful bride in my arms.

"We'll put the wedding on hold," she said, her breathing becoming rushed and a little erratic. "The deposits we can live without and…"

"No," I told her with a softness that I saved strictly for Riley. I released her arms and grabbed her face, forcing her to look at me. It seemed to calm her a little, slow down those spinning nerves. "This won't impact our wedding."

"Cam…" Something in her eyes told me. She knew. I had heard that women "just know" when their husbands strayed, like they had some kind of sixth sense. Only I hadn't strayed. Not physically.

At last, my hands dropped away. I turned from her, grabbed the Starbucks, and took a sip. It was getting cold, but it tasted just fine. I felt her hand on my shoulder.

"Cam," she said, the volume so low that her words barely carried above the crashing waterfall. "Let's just put it on hold. Until we figure things out."

When I faced her again, I let out a long breath. "Riley, there's something we need to talk about."

She gave me an understanding nod. Her face appeared numb.

Before we could speak a little more about it, Gordo came toward us, carrying his own box.

"Someone die?" he asked, laughing at his own words. He dropped the box, not delicately, and faced me. "You're not pissed that I told your fiancée about what went down, are you?"

I kept my eyes glued to hers, her unfaltering pupils laser-focused on me. When she looked away, I knew it was okay to face Gordo.

"No, it's all good," I admitted, letting out a long and tired sigh. "Are you all done?"

A 250-watt smile illuminated Gordo's face, and he rubbed his hands together like a child about to get himself into a whole world of trouble. When I glanced over at Riley, her frown suggested she was confused by Gordon's excitement at being newly unemployed.

"So…" I started, probably more confused like Riley than excited like Gordo. "What's next?"

He patted my back, right between my shoulder blades. "What's next is we go grab a few drinks. And fucking celebrate."

CHAPTER 29

With half of the day left to burn, I followed Gordo to the Chandler, a luxury condominium at the mouth of the Chicago River. He smiled the entire time, walking through the lobby and flashing a wink at the concierge who grinned back.

"Landon runs a commodities-based hedge fund," Gordo whispered once we boarded the elevator. He pressed the button for the 34th floor—there were thirty-six floors in total. "You know why I can't go home, right?"

I shrugged; I didn't really care.

The elevator doors opened, but Gordo didn't step forward. He grabbed my shoulders and gave me that look that he normally reserved for our strategy meetings. "Cam, if Melinda finds out I'm out of work, she's gonna sentence me to death." As the elevator doors began to shut, he flung his arm out and forced them open again.

"Sure, whatever you say," I said, stepping off the elevator before those doors could shut again.

"You've got a wedding coming up, your whole life ahead of you," Gordo went on, keeping his voice low as we walked down the long hallway toward one of only two doors. "You need to replace that income. And I need to find work, too. So follow my lead, okay? These are some good guys, and if you play things right, you'll have a solid set of friends. For life."

Before I could ask any questions, the door we were approaching opened, and a man in a suit and tie stepped out with a martini in one hand. He looked like a model with his dark hair, dark face, and unshaven jaw. I made a mental note to keep Hope away from this guy. And Riley, too.

"I thought my gay-dar was going crazy!" the guy sneered. Once we were close enough, he spread his arms and embraced Gordo, careful to not spill his drink.

"Landon," Gordo said, his voice tight with anxiety, "this is Cam, my protégé."

Landon winked; he was a good-looking dude. Even I felt special from the attention he gave me—which was just one glance, but still. Instead of a man-hug, though, he held out his hand.

"Pleasure to meet you," I said, allowing him to swallow my hand in his, shaking it with an elite firmness that suggested seven-figure bonuses and a Maserati for the daily commute. "Gordo has said some great things about you and your work."

Landon laughed, but it seemed forced and artificial. He waved us inside his condo. "What are you boys drinking? Markets are closing in a couple of hours and feeder cattle is up, up, up!"

Once inside, Landon hurried off to a crowd of other guys sitting and lounging on white leather sofas. Most drank from martini glasses, but a couple had bottles. Most wore suits; one wore a trader vest. There was white powder on the glass table, neither talcum nor sugar to rim those cocktail glasses.

"Jesus, Gordo," I whispered. "What the fuck is this?"

"Don't be shy, homos," Landon said, stepping up to what I assumed was a large bar. Later I realized it was his dining room table with every bottle and type of alcohol imaginable on it. "What's your poison on this glorious Monday afternoon, Gordon? Cam?"

Gordo nudged me forward. "Go with it. You'll be making two-fifty by the end of the month if Landon likes you." To Landon, he said, "Make mine one of those single malts you like."

Landon nodded, then shifted his attention to me. "And you? I can make you a daiquiri if you're thinking something fruity."

Fuck it. "I'll take whatever you're having."

The instant grin that rose on Landon's face allowed the sunlight from outside to reflect off his shining white teeth. "Your friend is my kind of guy, Gordon," he said, but kept his attention glued to me.

CHAPTER 30

The following afternoon, I made a few calls to some of Landon's friends in the financial services sector. Despite his bold and brash lifestyle—and his preference for male companionship—Landon was a decent guy. After the markets closed, we had a chance to talk about my area of specialization, how I could help a relationship-based organization, like a bank, know their clients so much better that they could make virtually any relationship profitable.

He seemed genuinely impressed. Then again, I certainly had the same awe in my eyes when he explained how humidity levels could impact the quality of grain that farmers fed their cattle, and as a result he needed to understand humidity so as to predict the price of feeder cattle futures.

After hanging up with one of Landon's key contacts—we'd had a good conversation with the promise of lunch in the coming weeks—I heard the doorbell. At first, it struck me as odd, but when I opened the door to find Gordo in a business suit and a big smile, I realized I should have expected this.

"Nap time's over, Cam," he said. "Get your shoes on. You need to see this car I'm going to buy."

I followed Gordo around like a good sidekick, jumping into

his BMW and driving out to the Tesla dealership, where he didn't even flinch at the $125,000 price.

"I want it," he said, then produced an Amex card. I recognized it as his corporate expense card from Harris, and wondered what was truly going on.

"I'm sorry, sir, we can't accept credit cards," the youngish salesman said.

Gordo laughed like it was no big deal. "I'll swing by with a bag of cash tomorrow."

"How about a cashier's check?" the salesman suggested with an arrogant smirk that told me he dealt with moneymakers like Gordon on a daily basis.

Once we left the dealership, Gordon told me he had a friend he wanted me to meet at the Burnham Park Yacht Club. "Josh ran the mortgage lending program at Wachovia before Wells took them out. He's still unemployed, but keeps busy with some of his other interests like slum-lording and futures trading."

I groaned, sliding a little deeper into the seat at the prospect of meeting yet another of Gordon's rich and spoiled friends who could easily be one line away from an overdose. "These guys are out of my league, Gordo. I just need a new job so I can get through this wedding."

He smacked my knee, a big smile on his face. "Me too. But Josh knows all the players. Tell him your story, and he'll have the decision-makers calling and offering you a job."

"I have to be home earlier tonight. Riley wasn't impressed

about last night." No, not impressed at all.

Gordo kept driving, but I watched his eyes blink while he steered the BMW through traffic. "How's that working for you, Cam? Two weeks ago, you were hanging out at the office and hoping for a chance meeting with this high school fling of yours."

"I love Riley," was my diplomatic, seasoned response.

Gordo liked that; he laughed. "Yeah, I love her, too. But really, how's it working out?"

I stared out the passenger window as we cruised down Lake Shore Drive.

"You know something, Cam?" Gordo said, his voice softer than I had remembered hearing it over the past few weeks. "Marriage takes a lot of work. It's like that shitty chinaware your mother wouldn't let you touch as a kid. One small nudge and it's broken."

I kept staring out the window, not really interested in what he had to say, but listening anyway because Gordo didn't listen to the radio while he drove unless it was Bloomberg.

"Sometimes you can fix those breaks, other times you can't. And hell, Melinda and I? We've broken ours a few times over."

That got my attention. I glanced over at him again, wondering what that meant, how that matrimonial china could get broken a few times over. If he noticed my prying interest all of a sudden, he didn't let on.

"Some of those breaks are fixed, others aren't. Luckily, none of those breaks has been fatal, but it's a chance we take. Like today, that Tesla I just bought? That might be the deal breaker." He chuckled like he didn't care, but I knew that, realistically, Gordo figured that if Melinda kicked his ass to the curb, he could turn up the charm and upsell her on a new and improved Gordo, the version that drove an electric vehicle.

So I chuckled, too. As a litigator, his wife wasn't the softest woman ever born, but she made bank, she looked great in a skirt, and Gordo seemed to drool every time she flashed him her killer smile. "Why are you telling me all this?"

He turned off Lake Shore and stopped at a traffic light, allowing himself to finally look at me. "You want to know how to make a marriage work? You don't give it a chance to break. There. It's that fucking simple."

This, coming from the guy who had just admitted to dropping and breaking that fragile marriage of his, seemed a little hypocritical. But that was Gordo. He seemed to want for me what he could not have for himself.

He hit the gas when the light turned green, and I told him that my being out with him these past couple of days was giving my marriage a chance to break. "And I'm not even married yet."

"Nah, this won't break the marriage." He glanced over me, his eyes surprisingly serious. "But that girl you've been waiting for? She will."

CHAPTER 31

Somewhere out in the middle of Lake Michigan, where we could no longer see the Chicago skyline, Josh killed the power and offered refreshments. He didn't drink alcohol, so neither Gordon nor I agreed to a beer; we all settled with a Diet Pepsi and dug into a bowl of nachos. The boat rocked with the waves, which were substantial enough to provide an explanation as to why so many people might get sick out here.

While Gordon and Josh talked about the latest theories on people management and the problems facing American financial institutions, I stared out at the vast body of water. To either side of this large 60-foot SeaRay Sundancer sport yacht, all I saw was the cold blue of the lake and followed it to where it met up with the warm blue sky at the horizon line. The sight inspired me.

As much as I wondered whether I would make it home early enough to have my heart-to-heart chat with Riley, I wished more than anything that Hope could be here on this boat with me. I imagined her smiling, sitting next to me, her hand edging toward mine on this white faux-leather bench, and her fingers brushing against my knuckles, teasing me.

I also remembered the dinner cruise scene from *Our Story,*

where Olivia and Oliver fell deeper in love. I hated that my thoughts focused on Hope instead of Riley, hated that—

"Right, Cam?" Gordo said, slapping me so hard on the back that I nearly spit the fantasy out of my mouth. "You're free this weekend for a boys' trip to the islands?"

I gave my best banker grin, held myself back from using my famous senior-manager word (which was "absolutely"), and instead shook my head. "Can't. We've got wedding stuff planned."

Gordo scowled, but Josh shrugged. "No worries. How about next weekend? You'll want to hang out with us; it's always a blast. My college roommate is the VP of analytics at Citigroup, and he'd love to have a mind like yours on his team."

Although next weekend didn't work either, I gave another banker grin and nodded this time. "Yeah, absolutely—" *Fuck, I said it, didn't I?* "—next weekend is perfect."

Handshakes and smiles all around.

Josh turned the captain's chair around and started the big diesel engines. Before leaning into the throttle, he turned and winked at me like all was good in the world.

CHAPTER 32

During the drive home, Gordon asked me where my attention had sailed off during our brief tour on the boat. "This is important shit, dickhead. I don't know if you noticed, but I'm not opening all of these doors for *me*. This is all you, all about finding *you* a job so you can get your shit straight with Riley."

His approach surprised me, catching me off guard. "Funny, I thought you needed me around to make sure you stayed out of trouble. Last night at Landon's, today on that big boat…what's your true angle here, Gordo?"

"You forgot the Tesla," he reminded me, chuckling but allowing it to fizzle out. "Once Melinda finds out what kind of severance package they gave me, she'll kill me." He glanced at me, slowing for the thick traffic up ahead. His eyes seemed to have a pleading quality to them. "Let me enjoy the next few weeks before my wife clues in and puts another crack in the chinaware of our marriage, okay? If you do that for me, if you let me have this brief time to myself, and in the process allow me to introduce you to some real big influencers in the industry, I'll make sure you're employed before your wedding day."

Gordon had never let me down, so I had no reason to distrust his words now. "But, Gordo? Why me?" He had his own problems, not to mention a huge electric bill to worry about.

We stopped. With rush hour congestion at its thickest, we weren't going anywhere very quickly. "Cam, you're at a turning point in your life right now. Whatever you decide over the next few weeks and months will determine your happiness level forever." We edged forward less than half a block, then stopped dead again. "I can't help you with Riley or this Hope girl, but I can help you with the career. Because after everything you've done for me and the others at Harris, setting you up with a new gig is the least I can do to show my thanks."

I couldn't help but smile, but then it sunk in, and I started laughing.

"I'm speaking from my heart, jackass," he said, feigning a broken heart as traffic opened up and the BMW reached thirty mph.

"Nah, you're speaking from your bank account. You know what Harris paid me—and yes, it was generous, even at my level—but better than all of that, you know what Harris paid *you*. And you know that the disparity between our pay-outs means you owe a few favors."

A momentary silence separated us, then Gordon started laughing. He laughed so hard that tears began pouring down his face, but once he managed to rein in the hysterics, he patted me on the leg.

No words were exchanged, but I knew it. I knew that whatever Harris had paid him to walk out of that office yesterday had been tremendous. In fact, it had been life-altering because guys like Gordo never signed an employment contract without the benefit of a termination clause that gave most people wet dreams.

PRESENT DAY

CHAPTER 33

11:12 AM

Arriving at Chuck's this early in the day affords us our choice of table. Because I once mentioned this place to Newman, I suggest something in the back, pointing to a U-shaped booth. The waitress doesn't object and within a few minutes, we're seated—Gordo across from me, and Hope between us in the booth's elbow, her back against the purple-satin wall. The combination of the restaurant's dim lighting and Hope's dark, almost-black hair makes her absolutely stunning in my eyes; her beauty captures my attention, something that Gordon notices right away.

His eyes jump between us as he assesses the situation. "Okay, lovebirds," Gordo says, clearing his throat. "You want to tell me what's going on today?"

I make an elaborate wave toward Hope, giving her the stage.

Gordon focuses on her. "Hope?" he asks. "Can you tell me what the fuck today is all about?"

A defiant smirk tickles the edge of her lips. She spares me a glance and says, "Told you I missed him." Then to Gordon, "I don't know." Then back to me, "I think that was a question for you,

Cameron. What is today all about?"

They both turn their attention to me. I shrug and shift my attention to Hope. "You know what I want out of this."

She consults Gordon. "I'm moving back out West next week, and—"

He nods, dismissing her words with an impatient wave that reminds me of his VP days at Harris. "I realize that. And I told him today was a bad idea. I told him it was a bad idea two months ago." He shakes his head. "Even after the huge fucking mess three years ago. Shit. So why don't you just tell him you're not into him? He needs to hear it." Gordon stares me down. "Cam, you need to let go of this bullshit. You married Riley, and you're chasing someone who will never love you."

In a soft voice, Hope quietly admits, "I love him, Gordon. I love him a lot."

It's the first time Hope has ever admitted to loving me. My head spins at the prospect of this day turning out the way I planned, another first when it comes to Hope.

Gordon slaps the table then growls one of his favorite words, "Fuck."

"But it doesn't mean I'm not moving—" Hope starts, but Gordon scoots out of the booth and motions at Hope and me to follow him.

"What is it?" I ask, concerned by how wide his eyes have grown.

Nodding past me, Gordo says, "It's Newman. He just

walked in. We need to get out of here."

Part of me wants to say, *fuck it*, but the realistic part of me understands that, with the recent shift in the value of our currency, if I don't keep my job, I have nothing left to pay the bills. Unemployed, with all of my capital in my condo, is a bad scene. So I automatically slide out of the booth before I even realize what I'm doing, and Hope is right there on my heels.

"Go," she urges behind me, giving me a soft shove. "He might've seen us."

I follow Gordon into the kitchen area. A few of the staff glance at us but don't overthink the situation—I'm guessing people make emergency exits like this all the time. I offer a few nods and smiles to the cooks, or whatever they're called. I don't see Chuck back here. I would recognize him because he gets quite the media coverage in the smaller, local publications.

As I chase Gordon outside, he launches into a semi-sprint, reaching North Michigan and heading left. There are more tourists north of the river, and I figure he plans on getting us lost among the crowds.

"Where are we going?" Hope asks, not exactly sprinting but walking pretty damn fast. I have to jog to keep up with her.

Gordon glances back as we reach the bridge, then eases up. "I think we're safe," he says, slightly out of breath.

For the first time since leaving Chuck's, I feel calm. Hope loves me, and that's all that really matters.

CHAPTER 34

11:23 AM

Gordon hates crowds. The farther north we walk, the antsier he seems to get. At the Water Tower building, he veers indoors, almost losing us. Hope and I share a glance like we used to, way back when, but follow him inside nonetheless. He heads to the escalators, stretching his arms into the air and rolling his head like he just played an intense game of basketball.

"Are you all right?" I ask him. On the second level, he points to a boutique clothing store.

"I need a bit of time," he admits. "Might grab a sweater or something, spend more of that severance. Give me a minute." He heads off in that direction, but stops and faces us, his forehead tight and stern. Using his finger for emphasis, he says, "Behave. Both of you. This isn't high school anymore."

I find Hope smirking once Gordon walks away. Alone with her, I start to ask the question that that has been itching at me since our interrupted lunch, but she recognizes the hurt and walks away before the words spill out.

"I love American Girl," she says, heading toward the second-level entrance of the American Girl store.

"If Gordo finds us sneaking off…" I start, glancing back toward the store where he ran off to for some "time." But I can't see him, and I realize that spending as much time with Hope as possible might actually help my plight.

I walk a little faster to catch up to her, but judging by how she speeds up as well, I'm starting to think she might not want to have this chat. So I start it anyway. "Back at the restaurant, what you said—"

She stops at a display and, with a nervous chuckle, asks me, "Isn't this crazy?"

I follow her attention to the display—an American Girl doll on a pony, wearing a helmet and horse-riding gear. Next to her stands another American Girl doll in coveralls and a plaid farmer's shirt. A third doll wears those tight pants, riding boots, and a whip. "It's the whip, isn't it?" I ask, suppressing my grin.

Hope punches me in the chest, followed by, "Cameron!" and walks to the next display. My pec muscle feels bruised, so I rub it to ease the pain before walking over to the next display with her—a sports themed one, all Chicago teams. But standing a safe two feet away this time, I take in all of her. She knows I'm close, I can *feel* her awareness, and it makes my heart beat a little faster. My hands ache for her like they have since that day at the airport after high school, since she walked away three years ago. I exist purely for Hope, and I'll never forget that because nothing I do will allow it.

I step closer and wrap my arms around her from behind,

fully expecting her to beat me away—hit me, kick me, scream—but she doesn't. She allows me to mold myself to her, to breathe in her coconut hair, and just live.

"At the restaurant," I try again, keeping my voice low, my lips close enough to her ear that she would feel the warmth of my words touching her skin.

"Stop, Cameron," she whispers her response. It sounds a little hesitant, like it still hurts or she's afraid. "I can't do this."

Rolling out of my embrace, she starts back toward the mall, but stops. When I reel around, I see why. Gordon stands at the entrance to American Girl Place, his hands on his hips. I don't know why he won't enter the store, but he doesn't.

"Come on," he says with a tone of defeat. "You two are supposed to be adults."

Hope exits the store, sidestepping Gordon and walking to the escalators that will take us down to the main level. Gordon doesn't move, though. He has a firm disappointment on his face.

"Cam, what are you doing?" He keeps his voice low so as to not make a scene. "Riley's all yours, she's everything you ever wanted. You married that girl for a reason. Do you remember that?"

I stare after Hope, anxiety pounding in my head at the fear that she might keep walking, that our sick day together might come to an early end. When I try to sidestep Gordo like she did, he stops me.

"Listen to me," Gordon says, firmer now, his eyes bulging with conviction. "You're going to regret this for the rest of your life. Let this bitch go."

I shake my head and shove past Gordon to hurry after Hope. "I can't," I tell him. Casting a backward glance at the only person who has ever truly stood by my side, I add, "This isn't my choice. She belongs here." I pat my heart, staring him down with the same conviction.

THREE YEARS AGO

CHAPTER 35

By Friday, Gordon had introduced me to a full Rolodex of people he knew throughout the financial services industry—guys he had gone to school with, friends of his family, associates from previous positions at other firms. I felt like his little brother, but the reality was that I couldn't keep up. I was exhausted, and I needed a break from the fast-paced lifestyle he led.

When Riley's alarm sounded, I groaned. She rolled out of bed, and I buried my head in her pillow. I didn't realize I had fallen back sleep until I felt her hand clawing up my back, her nails digging into my spine as a way to wake me up.

"Are you living like a rock star today?" she whispered into my ear, and the softness of her voice brought me to a place of instant peace. I imagined this was the same peace that someone who had quit smoking would find once he lights up again after years of breathing clean.

I rolled over and pulled her into bed with me, which earned me some playful laughter but nothing more. In her power suit, Riley looked as tasty as ever. I slid my hand inside her blouse, moving along her flat, soft belly. She smiled down at me, her eyes closing for a breath while I moved my hips against hers.

"Cam," she whispered as my other hand reached between her legs. She stopped me, and I realized that, like the person who donned Stanley's costume—the mascot for the Chicago Bears—once Riley stepped into her work attire, she was one hundred percent in character.

"I miss you," I admitted, sighing. I meant it, because with Riley, the range of emotions seemed constrained, manageable. The highs weren't too high, which meant the lows didn't drop too deep either.

She allowed a chuckle that sounded about as genuine as a two-headed quarter. "I'm sure the golfing yesterday has helped to numb that pain, huh?" Despite the bite of jealousy, she gave me a quick kiss, then backed out of bed, rolling the creases out of her suit as she stood above me. "So, what's on your and Gordo's travel itinerary today?"

I shook my head. "Nothing. I'm ignoring his calls and having lunch with Raj."

Her eyes twitched just enough that I detected her worry. "I don't know what's worse, you being away all week with no means to support the kind of lifestyle that your mentor leads, or having lunch with a serial cheater."

Touché. I chuckled. "First off, Gordo has been paying my way this week. He's pretending he wants me to connect with people who can get me a new job, but I know the truth. And secondly, Raj is not the kind of guy I would sleep with."

My joke lightened the mood a little. Still, Riley checked the time on her Gucci watch, then admitted that she needed to run. "But," she added, stopping at the bedroom door, her eyes a little dreamy and defeated. "We still need to talk about Hope and what she means to our wedding plans."

Hearing Hope's name on my fiancé's tongue felt blasphemous to my ears. It also gave me a sinking, drowning feeling because no matter how much I had tagged along with Gordon this week, I still had a lot of unfinished business with Hope. I had reread the story she emailed me last week, squinting to make out the words on my phone during those rare idle moments of watching the markets close at Landon's, docking at the yacht club on Josh's boat, waiting to clear customs in the Turks and Caicos islands for a day-long snorkeling (and drinking) excursion, and then again while sitting out on some of the more difficult holes at the golf course yesterday.

I loved and hated the story she had sent me because part of me believed that the few chapters were entirely *our* story, not something a woman named Emma Payne had written.

I snapped back to reality and discovered that Riley had slipped away without saying anything else, without the slightest indication she left. Once I heard the front door close behind her, I pulled the pillow back over my head and sought a little more sleep.

CHAPTER 36

Although we had planned on lunch, Raj preferred that we grab something quicker to eat, something we could take to-go and sit outside to eat. His suggestion surprised me because it was a warm day and he wore a jacket.

Rather than argue with him, I agreed, and we ordered our meals at the same Panera Bread that, in three years, would bring me face-to-face with the woman who would ultimately crush me. Of course, I didn't realize it at the time.

"So, where are we going to sit and eat?" I asked him, following him farther west.

He had a smirk on his face that made me wonder what his plans were. Riley's distrust for him didn't help. "There's this private and quiet spot right on the river." He winked at me. "You'll like it, I promise."

During the two-block walk, I asked Raj if he'd spoken with any employers recently, and he gave me a firm and decisive nod. "Between us, Second City Financial is replacing their VP of Human Resources."

Not even a full week had passed, and Raj already had a job

lined up. I suspected he hadn't had to build the connections like I had, either. Most likely Raj already had them.

"They could use someone like you, Cam," he said, and it didn't feel like his words were spoken out of pity. "The company needs to see some restructuring and growth. If you don't mind starting low on the ladder, let me know. I'll make sure you're looked after."

Unbelievable—the many faces I had met, courtesy of Gordon's introductions, flashed across my memory. None of them had offered to help me like Raj just had. It seemed they enjoyed partying, but felt I had to start in a C-suite level role because partying with a regular manager was frowned upon, slumming it.

"You appear disappointed, Cam," he said, frowning at me.

I swallowed the deliberation and gave him a thankful smile as we reached a stairwell that led down to the water. "No, not disappointed at all. I need this."

Raj waved me ahead of him. I climbed down the worn stairs that were a clear safety hazard and came to a small ledge a couple of feet above the water. The landing was large enough to accommodate a bistro table, but not much else. And of course, there was no bistro table—just the ledge. Raj removed his jacket and laid it on the ground like a picnic blanket. There wasn't a whole bunch of room left for me to sit on the jacket, so half of my ass stayed clean and the other half would need to be brushed of the dust and dirt.

"Have you enjoyed your week, Cam?" Raj asked me, opening the sandwich wrapper in his lap and taking a healthy bite.

I told him about my adventures with Gordon. "And you?"

"Heartbreaking, actually." He let out a sigh and hung his head. "Remember Katja?"

The Russian beauty who worked in the mailroom at Harris and made most men smile. Between her Eastern European accent, fine looks, and skimpy outfits, she could make a priest smile. How could anyone forget about Katja?

"Well, we broke up," he said with a shrug. "I really loved that one. She had the tightest—"

I nearly choked, interrupting Raj from finishing his thought. He handed me my bottled water, which I sipped and confessed to him that I didn't know he and Katja were in a relationship. "I thought you were married."

He nodded. "I am. But, Cam, sometimes one woman can't satisfy all of your needs." Some kind of memory put a super-big smile on his face. "Katja really, really satisfied me." And then the smile disappeared, and he shrugged again. "I love my wife, but we do not…" he seemed to search for the right word, "… I will say we do not 'connect' on certain things that are vital in a marriage."

I didn't know what that meant, but I knew that Raj's wife was an amazing, kind, and gentle woman. She often cooked delicious ethnic dishes and desserts for the group at Harris, and she remembered my name, which always made me appreciate her. But the other reason I had lost focus on the conversation about Raj's infidelities was that I saw Hope across the river, on the patio overlooking the water.

"Marriage isn't an easy thing," Raj continued, but I barely heard the words as I rose off the jacket, still staring across the water.

"Sometimes you do whatever it takes to make it work, and in that quest, you find yourself between another woman's…Cam, what are you doing?"

Climbing the stairs two at a time, my eyes remained locked on Hope. She was sitting at a table with another man, probably eating lunch as well. I could tell she wore a skirt, her long legs a beautiful sight, even from this distance. I missed those legs, missed the taste they left on my tongue, and suddenly my hunger shifted to a more voracious one.

"Cam!" he shouted, but his voice seemed distant, like four-blocks-away distant when he was really only a stone's throw down and back.

Halfway across the bridge, I chanced a glance back at Raj's secret nook. "Sorry, Raj. I'll call you later."

He chuckled with a what-the-fuck-just-happened confusion on his face.

Sprinting the rest of the way across the iron bridge, I noticed that the lunch between Hope and this much older man was probably one neither of them wanted interrupted. Was this her live-in boyfriend?

The geriatric fuck reached under the table and put his hand on her knee, squeezing it. It killed me to see that, but then she swatted him away. He laughed, and she didn't seem impressed. I felt better about that; it meant I wouldn't have to embarrass him too much.

In fact, as I came closer, I wondered what I had planned to do in the first place. *What am I doing here?*

My sprint slowed to a casual walk as I approached their table.

Now within earshot, the geriatric dickhead looked up from Hope, and we made eye contact while he was mid-sentence. He kept talking, though, and Hope didn't bother to glance back. He was good, the kind of guy who could have dinner with his wife and eye-fuck the waitress without anyone knowing.

I kept walking past their table, my heart pounding in my chest. *Shit, shit, shit.* Taking a deep breath, I glanced back over my shoulder. Hope saw me. She recognized me. And unlike her slick lunch date, she wasn't so good at eye-fucking without getting noticed. The old dude obviously noticed that Hope's attention had strayed, so he turned around in his chair and looked as well. But by then, I had faced forward and just kept going.

At the next street, I stopped and deliberated. *Deep breath.* I glanced back and noticed that Hope's smile had gone away and, for a moment, I hated myself for that. I checked on Raj across the river, saw him eating his sandwich. Somehow he could see that I was looking his way, so he offered a friendly wave. Shaking my head, I ignored him and turned toward the building.

The entrance on this street was not as elaborate as the other entrance, the one that overlooked the terrace, but it would work just fine. Stepping inside, I looked around. There was a café a little farther up, stairs to the mezzanine level, a bunch of elevators closer to the other entrance. I decided on the café and purchased a bottle of water to help with my suddenly dry mouth. By the time I paid the cashier, I noticed that Hope and the geriatric fucktart were holding hands and waiting for an elevator.

The geriatric fucktart didn't see me, but I knew Hope had. Not that her eyes found me, but she seemed to be focusing really hard on not noticing me. Even though her eyes refused to shift in my direction, I knew she sensed me. Because I could sense her.

"Sir?" a man asked. The voice came from behind me.

I didn't want to take my eyes away from Hope, as if I knew she would be gone by the time I could return to her. But I did, and it felt as painful as ripping a Band-Aid from your forearm.

"Your change," the man said, handing me the eighteen dollars in change for the bottled water. He smiled like he had just saved my retirement from the market collapse of a few years ago.

"Thanks," I said, hiding my annoyance about being distracted. Sure enough, when I glanced back toward the elevators, Hope and her grandfather were gone. *Shit.*

I hurried toward the elevator bank where I had last seen them and stared at the numbers. There were four shafts—one stopped at thirty-eight, the next at twenty-nine, the third at thirty-seven, and the fourth at fifteen. None of the elevators were moving, so I memorized each floor.

Then I waited. Determined to find Hope, I boarded the first elevator and rode up to the 38th floor, but it was nothing but security cameras and closed doors. I walked around to the bathroom so I didn't look too suspicious to the attentive folks watching the cameras, washed my hands, splashed water in my face, then rode down to the 37th floor.

This floor was an accounting firm with a smiling receptionist to greet me.

"Is this KPMG?" I asked, stepping toward the counter and putting my best charming smile on my lips.

She swiveled in her chair and waved at the company's large, blatant sign— Lankin, Halpern, Norris & Associates. When she came back to me, she blinked so hard that I swore it was Morse code for "Are you illiterate?"

"Oh, sorry," I said. As I turned to walk away, I felt it—a skipped heartbeat of sorts—before I even noticed Hope stepping into the lobby area from another set of doors.

The receptionist noticed how my attention hovered on Hope a little longer than it should have, unless we knew one another. When Hope caught me standing at the reception desk, she made sure to ignore me even though her geriatric companion wasn't accompanying her.

Without wanting to draw unwanted attention to myself, I focused on the receptionist again and asked, "Is KPMG in this building?"

Still with that patronizing smile, she shrugged. "It's possible they are among the fifty or so tenants, but you'd have to check with the directory downstairs."

As much as I wanted to strangle her for her patronizing nature, I heard the elevator *ding* behind me. "Thank you," I said, then hurried to catch the elevator, but the doors were already closing.

I watched Hope stare straight back at me, unmoving as the gap between those doors narrowed. As a grin surfaced on her face, I hated her for letting those doors close without me on board with her.

With just an inch or less to go for those doors to shut, there was another *ding* and the doors re-opened. I hadn't pressed the button—wasn't close enough to—but saw that Hope had pressed the OPEN button at the last possible instant.

"Heading down, sir?" she asked with the polite tone of a complete stranger.

"Thank you," I said, blinking hard as my heart pounded in my chest.

She held the door as I boarded, not acknowledging me. Even though there was nobody else on the elevator, I did the same and when I regained my bearings I noticed some sort of recognition on the receptionist's face. Did she see the history between Hope and me? Could she sense the tension, the love, whatever the fuck this really was?

Once the doors eased shut, Hope punched me in the arm. Hard. "What are you doing here?" she hissed, stepping closer to me, then shoving me backward against the elevator wall. It wasn't an affectionate shove either.

I fumbled for the right words. "I…I saw you…"

She shoved me again, her lips tight and one mistake away from an outright, teeth-baring sneer. "*He* saw you! He fucking saw you!"

"Hope," I begged as she shoved me again. This time, I seized her wrists. She normally hated that, but this time, I pulled her hands down to her side, forcing her to step closer to me. Our bodies were so close, I swore I could feel her body heat radiating through mine. The wrist-restraining also calmed her.

I edged closer to her, our faces inches apart so that when I breathed, her hair danced gently around her jaw. "I see *you*," I said. "I see you everywhere. I can't stop seeing you." I shook my head, averting my eyes for less than a second. When I found her again, her hands moved to my face.

She was forceful—not quite hungry or desperate, but forceful—as she seized my face and pressed her lips against mine. My mouth opened for her tongue, and I tasted her. Whatever hunger was missing earlier suddenly surged through my body. It was the same awakening as when we kissed on the grass, arousing the realization that I had missed her without ever admitting to it.

I stepped forward, forcing Hope back against the opposite wall with enough of a *thud* that the entire compartment rattled along its tracks. I didn't know whether we were thirty floors from the lobby, or two…I didn't care.

With my right hand, I reached down and grabbed her left, the one with the big shiny engagement ring, and pinned it above her head.

She wrapped her leg around my waist and pulled me closer, definitely feeling my erection pressing against her as she moaned, "Oh, Cameron."

I nearly lost it as she suggestively rolled herself against me.

Reaching down, I put an end to this short dry-humping, sliding my hand past the waist of her panties, deeper, through the short hair that she still kept in a narrow landing-strip formation and between her warm lips.

"Cameron," she breathed, pulling her mouth away from mine and burying her face. My middle finger massaged her clit before reaching even farther south and dipping into her, just a shallow taste on my fingertip. "Oh, fuck," she said, then either bit down on my neck or sucked on it, hard.

The elevator came to a stop, and I jumped back against the opposite wall. I watched Hope, her face flushed with the hint of perspiration at her hairline. She shuddered and grabbed the railing for support.

A trio of men in suits stepped aboard, none of them paying much attention to either of us. When Hope turned her attention back to me, I very deliberately lifted my middle finger to my lips and despite the way she shook her head—*don't you dare*, she seemed to warn me—I savored the taste of her in my mouth. Her eyes rolled back as she turned her attention away.

My little display did nothing to lighten the tension between us, not to mention the discomfort in the crotch of my pants.

CHAPTER 37

We stepped outside, the sun beating down on us. Although it was the same patio as before, the world felt foreign to me now that Hope was there to enjoy it with me. Neither of us spoke, but we shared a glance before she laced her hand in mine and took off sprinting, nearly ripping my arm out of its socket.

She laughed, knowing she'd caught me off-guard, and it was infectious. Her giddiness reached deep down into my stomach, filling me with a satisfaction I could only describe as hope. All this time without Hope felt like wasted worry all of a sudden. I had written her off, written off this very feeling as the final fairy tale, the stuff of Easter Bunnies and Santa Claus, the one piece we cling to as humans and, even as adults, are reluctant to let go. That final piece was *this*; it was the kind of true love that Hope had dismissed in her poem all those years ago. But it existed, and it was real. It was *us*. She was my soul mate, my air; it wasn't a lie.

We crossed the river, and I glanced toward the little spot where Raj had brought me for lunch. He was gone now, and the spot looked lonely, abandoned.

"Where are we going?" I asked as we sprinted past the Opera House.

She glanced back, her eyes projecting nothing but common-sense honesty. "My hotel."

"I'm supposed to be getting married in—" even to my own ears, the response sounded rehearsed.

"Cameron," she said, stopping for a traffic light and taking my face with her hands again. She gave me a crooked grin that revealed all of her insecurities and scars, all of her beauty in the flash of an instant. "You can't touch me like you did in that elevator and think I'm going to pretend this doesn't exist between us anymore."

And then she kissed me before our light turned green.

She darted off again, and I struggled to keep up with her, wondering the entire time whether people thought we had just robbed a bank in our designer clothes, trendy shoes, and stupid-big smiles on our faces as we made our way to her hotel.

Once we entered the uptight lobby, the desk clerk shot her a careful glare.

"Welcome back, Miss McManus," the clerk said as Hope pulled me past the desk. "We thought you were…"

We didn't hear the rest of what he said because we had already boarded the next elevator. With a trembling finger, Hope pressed the button for the tenth floor. During the very short and quick ascent, we didn't kiss, and we barely touched. We simply stared and smiled at each other, two high school kids stuck in their twenties with the complications of their respective relationships standing between them, their hands brushing, their glares tentative.

She mouthed the words, "I want you," then started to pout in that teasing, seductive way that only Hope could pull off. I wanted her, too, wanted those pouty lips on mine so badly that I ached for them. But when I closed my eyes and leaned in for a kiss, she pushed me away.

The doors opened. Taking my hand, she led the way to her room, a few doors down on the left. The room had a nice view of the Chicago River, the bridges joining the north and south sides of the city before the water branched left and right in the distance. Standing there, I knew that I would remember this room forever, just like I remembered our first time, our last time, and all the times in between—in the car, my bedroom when my parents were out, the basement of her parents' house while we pretended to watch movies underneath a heavy blanket…

Despite the familiarity between us, it had been such a long time. My gut churned with the anticipation of loving her again.

Hope reached down to my waist and unbuckled my pants, tugging them down to my knees before reaching into my boxers and stroking me softly. Her hand felt soft against my rigid, throbbing shaft. She had that perfect touch, and at just the right moment, she lowered herself to the floor and took me in her mouth.

I didn't realize that my eyes had rolled back until I couldn't see anything but the blackness on the inside of my eyelids. Even then, Hope's face seemed to beam back at me through that darkness.

It didn't take long for the hunger from the elevator to return.

And it was ravenous. Snapping back to reality, I reached down and somehow scooped her up into my arms. She didn't yelp or protest. Instead, she wrapped her arms around my neck, one hand brushing through my hair until she secured a firm grip. Tugging at my hair, she angled my face toward hers, and I lost myself in her hazel eyes. I remembered that stare—it was knowing and lost at the same time.

She kissed me, her own insatiable hunger back as well. Like that day on the wet grass, only unrestrained like back in high school.

Lowering her onto the bed, I fumbled to get her out of her shirt, but she refused to stop kissing me. She wrapped her legs around me again, locking me against her with a firm and unmistakable strength.

"I miss you," I whispered, pulling my mouth from hers long enough to refill my lungs with air and to slide her shirt over her head.

My hands found her breasts, my fingers circled her hard nipples, and then I pinched them lightly, but hard enough to make her feel the slightest amount of pressure.

She let out a soft moan. "Cameron…" she pleaded.

"I want to lick your face," I said, the words slipping out of my mouth without my knowledge.

"I'll cut you if you try." It was the softest threat I had ever heard, and it made my dick throb.

While my lips kissed a path along the vein at side of her neck, across her collarbone—she always loved that—and down to those hard nipples, my hand slipped into her panties. Hope spread her legs a little wider, just enough for me to notice. She wanted me touching her. I continued to massage her clit, picking up where I had been forced to let go in that elevator.

I felt her heart beating erratically beneath her chest, her breathing deepening. She grabbed my free hand and brought it to her mouth, sucking gently on my fingers.

"Oh, Cameron," she continued, her eyes rolling back like they had in the elevator, only this time I watched them disappear behind her closed eyelids. She gave herself to me.

My tongue licked a path past her navel, and I drew my hand from her mouth. Glancing up her body, I caught her staring at me, her cheeks rosy once again, her teeth biting down on her lip. I watched her as I unzipped the back of her skirt and pulled it off. I hooked my fingers around her black, lacy panties, but when I glanced back at her face for approval, she shook her head. No.

"Hope," I begged. When I started tugging at her panties, she stopped me, so I took her leg with my hand and circled my tongue around the inside of her knee, still watching her as she slammed her head back, exposing the length of her neck.

Moving along the inside of her thigh, she stopped me when I reached her moist core, my tongue tracing along the elastic of those panties.

"No, Cameron," she said, her voice hitched. She gripped my hair again, this time using force.

"What?" I asked, bringing my fingers to her clit and massaging her again before we engaged in a staring contest.

"You're going to make me come," she remarked, her voice

hitching.

I nodded. *Duh, wasn't that the point?*

She shook her head again. "I want us to come together."

Using her feet and legs, she peeled me out of my pants and boxers, exposing me. Hovering above her, she pulled me down onto her, releasing my hair and using her hand to stroke my shaft once, twice. I loved how gently she worked me. I stared down and watched her hand guide me toward her wet, wanting pussy. Once I knew I was close enough, I tried to edge myself inside her, but she stopped me.

Shifting my attention, I asked, "What's wrong?"

And that was when she returned to me, the version of Hope I had known for all of those years. The beautiful and perfect Hope who I had loved so fiercely, the one I would never stop loving. It was the vulnerable and pure Hope.

"I still love you," she said, her eyes tearing up.

"I've never stopped, never will," I promised, making sure she knew I wasn't fucking around.

When her hand left my shaft, I reached down and pressed the tip against her moist lips.

"Love me, Cameron," she pleaded, her eyes closing and her mouth jumping at mine. We kissed hard, lost in the thrusts, my hands gripping hers so fiercely that my fingers went numb.

"I love you, Hope," I moaned, and she knew what that meant.

Somehow, she was straddling me now, grinding her hips against mine, and she held my hands above my head, her hair in my face. "Look at me," she said, her short and rapid breaths in my face.

I opened my eyes, found hers. She smiled as best she could given the increasing speed of my movement.

"Look at me when you come inside me, Cameron."

I fought to keep my eyes open so I could see her complete abandon, the emotion building up in her face. She came first, her muscles tightening, convulsing against my shaft. She moaned and fought the urge to close her eyes against the ecstasy of her orgasm.

Watching her, feeling her come against me…it spelled my end as well. Arching my neck back, I fought the urge to release.

"Cameron!" she moaned, her muscles still contracting. She grabbed my face and forced me to look at her, her hips moving fast and hard. "I… I…" She moaned again.

At last, I came, my eyes locked on hers the entire time.

Collapsing on my chest, Hope rested her head on the pillow next to mine.

"Don't leave me, Cameron," she whispered, spent and exhausted. "Please don't ever leave me again."

CHAPTER 38

The Ferris wheel on Navy Pier that night allowed a spectacular view of the city lights, the shores of Lake Michigan, and all the way into the darkness behind us. As the wheel climbed upward, the street-level sounds dimmed, allowing just the hush of the breeze to roll across us.

Hope rested her head on my shoulder, her hand wrapped in mine. I closed my eyes as she snuggled into me, realizing that in a few weeks' time, I would have become a married man if Hope hadn't shown up. I didn't know how I should feel about what had happened today, about how our life together meant such drastic change for her old man (literally) and Riley. No matter how right it seemed in my heart, I was pretty certain that my ex-fiancée would not see things this way.

But at this moment in time, nothing else mattered. Not the nuptials I had to cancel, not even Riley's feelings. All that mattered was Hope's head on my shoulder, her hand in mine, her warmth against me.

"Why did you disappear, Cameron?" she asked.

Her voice forced my eyes open. I nuzzled my nose into her

hair and breathed her in, hoping to stain my lungs with her essence because I wanted her with me forever. But even that evening, riding the Ferris wheel with Hope, I knew our time together would not last. Two heartbeats ago, I had accepted walking away from Riley and our wedding date. But I *felt* that Hope would not allow me to.

"I came here to find you, Cameron," she continued, her words filled with ache. "And I found that you were living a happy life with a pretty woman who would keep you happy. That's all I needed to see. I could've let go. But now…now I want to know again. I don't care if you're happy with Riley. I don't care if she's where your days begin and end." She let out a sigh and pulled her head off my shoulder. After studying me for a beat, she kissed me, hard, and it happened in-sync with the wheel making its next upward climb. I felt like I was flying.

"I love you," I said when she pulled back. "I don't want to go home, I want to stay here forever."

"I'm here," she said. "And I don't want you to go home. But if you don't tell me why you disappeared, you'll never see me again. I can't keep beating myself up over this."

I nodded, understanding. "I didn't want the hurt. I didn't want to know how you dealt with our goodbye. I know what *I* did and how I dealt with your absence. I know that my first semester was a dry one, and I lost a bit of weight and hated how life looked without you."

She remained silent, listening to my words without interrupting me.

"But then I found Riley, and she filled those gaps." I felt my throat constricting. "I love her for that, for bringing color back into my days and for reminding me that I could smile. She's pretty and smart, and she replaced everything you were to me. She was that piece that made my life worthwhile. If life were a battery-operated gadget, she was my battery, just like you were. So without you around, I turned to Riley. She wasn't a replacement, or at least she didn't feel like one. She was just…her. I rediscovered what happy meant because of her."

As much as I hated sharing all of this with Hope, I could tell, by the way her mouth hung open, that hearing my words stung. A lot. I wondered if she regretted pushing me into this confession in the first place.

"I could've walked away at any time, just like it felt like you walked away from me after you left me that poem," I continued, the Ferris wheel making its final approach to the loading platform. "But I couldn't. I couldn't walk away from Riley because I was afraid of finding you with your own male version of my happiness." I took a deep breath for courage. "Like seeing you today with that old guy."

I searched her eyes for a hint. Why did she have a hotel room all to herself when the guy who put a ring on her finger was right here in Chicago? What was Hope's real story? What was she doing in Chicago after all these years? Why hadn't she left yet when she told me she would only be here until this week?

"I don't want to go home tonight, Hope," I confessed, squeezing her hand. Part of me feared she might take a swing at me, but she didn't. Instead, her hand remained limp in mine. "My time without you has killed me, absolutely killed me. I've split my heart into two these last seven years."

The ride operator greeted us with a smile and opened the door to let us off. We weren't quick to get up and disembark, but I took the lead and Hope followed.

"Where to?" I asked.

She gave a dismissive nod toward the far end of the pier that protruded out to Lake Michigan. There were a few people walking to that end, promising a bit of privacy so we could finish talking about this. So I led her that way, giving her hand another quick squeeze.

"Cameron," she said, her voice beaten and worn down all of a sudden. "Tell me about these dual hearts."

I took a deep breath, nodding. "I had one part of my heart that existed for the life that Riley gave me. It wasn't the life of happiness I had envisioned for myself, wasn't the life that you're giving me. But it was a life. It was just one small part of me, of my heart." I heaved a deep breath. "The other part of my heart, though? It's the part reserved for you, for all of the perfection and *living* that you made possible, that you promised. And that's what it is; it's my hope. The hope that you will find me, just like you have. The hope that you will love me always, just like you do."

"But I can't," she whispered across the soft gusts coming off the lake.

I stopped her and pulled her into a tight embrace. I let her melt into me before continuing. "You can't stop this love, Hope. You can fight it and bury it, but you can't stop it. Trust me."

"Stop," she said, gripping me tighter. "Stop talking."

I felt her hand sliding up my back, tightening between my shoulders before settling at the base of my skull.

"I can't," I told her, my eyes burning now. "Just like I couldn't bury you in my past. Because no matter how much you belonged there, no matter how much I wanted to banish you to that dark compartment of memories and sadness, I just couldn't. I tried."

"Cameron," she whispered, her voice cracking. "You're killing me."

"You're here, Hope, and I'm here. We're together like we're supposed to be." I pulled her away from me, so she could see the tears in my eyes, and I could see the tears in hers. "I don't know what I'm supposed to do," I confessed. "I love Riley, I swear I love her."

When one of those tears rolled down her face, I leaned in and kissed it away. I would've kissed those tears away for the rest of my life, if only she would allow me.

"Cameron," she said, blinking and setting free several more tears. "I know you don't love her like you love me."

I shook my head. "No. I don't, Hope. And I'm afraid that if you and I walk away from this, we walk away from…" I stared up at the sky, the stars, and moon. "If we walk away, we leave everything. And that's not how I want to live, Hope. I can't have two halves of one life. One that belongs exclusively to you, and the other that belongs to the hope of replacing you. I can't…I can't…exist without you."

She stared off, back toward the crowds. I figured she might be searching for an escape into *her* other life, the half that had allowed her to move on. The half that must've broken two weeks ago when she showed up outside my townhouse in the pouring rain.

She allowed a grin, but it flickered on her lips so quickly that anyone else would've questioned its very existence. But I caught it. Not because I had perfect 20/20 vision either. I felt that smile in the form of a skipped heartbeat.

"Don't make me go home tonight," I begged.

When her eyes found mine again, she nodded. I didn't know what it meant, though. Was she nodding because I *had* to go home, or did she want me to stick around?

"Talk to me," I begged.

"I can't," she whispered. "If I talk, I'll lose everything I came here for."

When I opened my mouth and started to speak, she placed a finger over my lips to silence me.

Leaning forward, she brought her mouth to my ear, and in a broken whisper, she asked, "Take me back to the hotel. Love me. Remember me. And then tell me whether or not you exist for me."

"I don't need to make love to you to know that, Hope. All I need is to take a breath of you."

"Then breathe me, all of me," she begged. "In my hotel room."

CHAPTER 39

Sometime around two am, I woke up with Hope curled around me underneath the hotel bed's sheets. I stared up at the ceiling, trying to orient myself. I couldn't see Hope's face, and although that caused brief panic, I realized that I wasn't aching for Hope like I had in the past. She was right there with me. And for the first time since I could remember, I felt whole again.

Then I heard it again, the bleep of a police siren, and I wondered if Hope's geriatric fiancé or Riley herself had sent the police for me. Of course neither of them had, but those were the kinds of fears I had at two in the morning, after falling asleep with my soul mate in my arms.

Sliding out of bed, I picked our clothes up off the floor and flung them on the chair in the corner. I grabbed my phone to discover that I had missed six calls while it was on silent. The call register showed that all of them had come from either my home number or Riley's cell. There were several texts, too, but I didn't bother counting them or looking at them. I didn't want the guilt.

Locking the screen, I tossed the iPhone onto the heap of clothes and cast a glance at Hope while she slept peacefully on the bed before walking to the bathroom, naked and a little raw from my night with her.

I closed the door as quietly as possible, hit the lights, and stood at the mirror. My reflection surprised me because it had a foreign familiarity, like when you don't see someone for a long time but there they are, standing right in front of you. You *know* that face, you *know* that person, but it takes a moment or so for the walls to fall and for you to open your arms.

Grinning, I realized this was what my life had been all about. I remembered this emotion, this immortality. I had known it fairly well in high school and the months leading up to my trip to Chicago, where I would try to bury this feeling deep down and never allow it to ruin my mind again.

It was called love, and this feeling happened only with Hope. Without Hope, I would never know love like this again.

Still staring at my reflection, I had my answer.

I knew what had to be done.

And my life, I realized, would be the happiest life anyone could ever imagine.

CHAPTER 40

Crawling back into bed behind Hope, I saw that she had rolled over while I was in the bathroom. I snuggled up behind her, slipping my arms around her chest, her nipples brushing against the inside of my forearms.

"Second thoughts?" she mumbled.

"You're my first thoughts, my only thoughts," I whispered back, burying my face in her dark hair. I loved the smell of Hope.

"What will happen once you go back?" she asked, her voice warming up to the conversation.

"I don't know," I admitted. Despite my confessions last night at Navy Pier, I didn't want to think about Riley right now. She didn't deserve this, not now. Not three weeks prior to her wedding day, not ever. "You?"

Instead of answering me, Hope rolled over so that her face came within inches of mine. I adored this woman, every little detail, every inch and ounce of her. I reached out, extending the same hand that had slipped into her panties earlier, the hand that I blamed for tonight. My fingers traced her jawline all the way to her chin.

"When I close my eyes, all I see and hear is you, Hope. Now I want to memorize how you feel, your soft face, these lines, and—" I stopped at the scar on her chin, "—and the blemishes." I leaned in and kissed her chin, then had to fight the hunger to take her again. I moved my tongue along her neck, just for a taste.

"Cameron," she said. It wasn't her turned-on tone, so I stopped tasting and stared into her eyes to see what was wrong. "What are we doing?"

Her question made me uncomfortable. I shifted as a way to escape the mild pain. "This isn't wrong, Hope."

She frowned at me like I had just insulted her. "I didn't say anything about it being wrong. I just asked what are we doing here."

"This is us." I twirled her hair with my fingers. "It's what I've wanted from the moment I met you. Two weeks ago, when I saw you outside my townhouse in the rain, it came back to me. I love you, Hope. And you love me."

Her eyes danced from one side of my face to the other, surely testing the truth in what I had just told her.

"What we're doing is starting all over again," I explained like it made the most perfect sense in the world.

"This is what I wanted years ago," she said, her face twisting with hesitation. "Now? It's too late, Cameron. We had our shot, but we fucked up. I fucked up. You fucked up." The pain in her words told me she believed her words. Or if she didn't believe them, then she would fight pretty damn hard to make sure she believed them.

I had no response but a half-grin that came from that other part of my heart, the part *not* reserved for Hope.

"Don't be sad," she said, the tears from earlier coming back with a sudden ferociousness. Her hand slid across the sheets to find mine. "I never fought, Cameron. Maybe I should've. Maybe I should've taken that upon myself to fight for this love. And I blame myself."

"Don't," I told her, throwing her words back. "You don't believe in fighting for love."

"I might not believe in fighting for love," she admitted, "but I believe in fighting for you, Cameron."

I bit down on my lip. Her words were sweet, but I refused to shed a tear.

Hope didn't have the same luck; she cried for a bit, so I held her, let the warm tears roll across my chest on their way to the bed sheets. I hated her sadness; they contradicted the strength that defined her. And in that instant, the lost time of the last seven years became incredibly real. It was wasted, irrevocably lost, and it allowed me a glimpse into the future.

I saw Hope as an old woman, grey hair and a face that, while wrinkled and a little droopy, remained the most beautiful sight my eyes would ever behold. I saw the vibrancy of her spirit, despite the frailty of her age. And, more important than any physical restrictions that time seemed to be imposing on us, I saw what true love was all about. Her beliefs were wrong. And I couldn't let the next seven crucial years—or seventy, for that matter—escape us.

"I fucked up, Hope," I confessed, admitting to her as much as to myself. "But I'm here now." I reached down and nudged her chin upward so I could kiss her mouth. "I'm here," I promised.

She sobbed a little longer before falling asleep in my

embrace. Despite the loss of sensation in my hand and arm, sensing Hope's ease while she dozed against me only reinforced why I seemed to be sacrificing so much just to be here with her. I loved her.

This moment made the loss of the past seven years seem strangely worthwhile. Because here we were—the next seven would make up for it, and we were so lucky to have found each other now so that we could realize our mistake and take advantage of the years ahead of us. Now that we knew how important this was, there was no way we would ever let go.

Right?

Yes.

That morning in the hotel room, with her dried tears on my chest, was the first and only time I ever forgave myself for allowing life to ever exist without her.

CHAPTER 41

Sunday morning, after being away from Riley all weekend, I woke with a headache. Rolling out of bed, I poured myself a glass of water in the bathroom. When I returned to the sleeping area, I found Hope sitting up in bed, the television tuned in to The Weather Channel, her knees pulled up to her chest. The lack of focus in her face indicated she wasn't exactly listening or paying attention to the long-term forecast.

"Do you have Aspirin or Tylenol?" I asked. "I have a headache."

She shook her head.

I sat on the edge of the bed and watched her. The sight of her distracted me from the pounding in my head, but it also worried me because this wasn't the woman I had made love to all weekend. This wasn't the woman I had spent hours shopping with yesterday, laying on the grass in Millennium Park, listening to live music with at some of the best blues clubs around, and later drinking martinis with at the finest bars that Gordo had introduced me to. This was a girl borne of heartbreak, the Hope I had found outside my condo in the rain, the broken and insecure Hope I had expected after all of these years.

"Where does this end for us?" she asked at last, easing her eyes from the television and staring at me, bold and serious.

"Does it have to end?" I replied.

"I'm flying back to Miami on Wednesday," she said, her quiet voice coming apart. "It has to end. There's no other ending to this story of ours."

"No." I shook my head, arousing my headache from its dormant state so it could throb back to life, reminding me that I still hadn't found a solution to the pain. I crawled closer to Hope, kissed her knees through the sheets, and studied those pained, hazel eyes.

"I'm sorry, Cameron," she whispered.

"No," I insisted. "We can make this work. We'll make it happen. What are the chances fate brought us back together? Here? Now? There's a reason for it. We need to act on it before it's lost."

"You're getting married," she groaned, turning her back to me and curling up on the bed.

I slid in behind her, pulling the sheet up over her back for some reason I didn't quite understand, and then wrapped my arms around her. "Hope, I can't get married. That's crazy. And I'm convinced that's why you're here. It's why I'm here. The timing isn't something either of us controlled."

She shook her head. "What's marriage to you, Cameron?"

I shrugged, more for myself because she wouldn't see it, because I was unable to give her an answer. I knew what I *wanted* it to represent. But that ideology involved Hope, not Riley. "I want *us*, Hope. I want to wake up like this, minus the sad thoughts, but…*this*." I squeezed her, embraced the weight of her against me. "Being here with you, being able to hold you, kiss you in the morning, do the things we did yesterday, the day before, and yeah, the *sex* is amazing, too. But *this* is what marriage should be. Don't you think? Shouldn't marriage be love?"

Although I couldn't see her face, I knew she had closed her eyes super tight and was weeping ever so faintly in my arms.

"And if marriage is about love," I continued, because I really needed her feel this, to want it and never let it go, "doesn't that mean it should be about *us*?"

Her subtle quaking subsided, and she wiped her face with her hands, eliminating the evidence of tears. "Where are the goals in that, Cameron?"

"Goals?" I reached out and tucked her hair behind her ear, kissing the exposed skin of her neck, that one spot where the vein would pulsate and tell me so much about her moods.

"Yes," she insisted with the edge of heartbreak. "Marriage is just two people with one common goal. Remember? It's what I believe."

My heart ripped at those words, at her refusal to let go of those crazy beliefs from so long ago. I thought of other married people—my parents, my friends, even Gordo and his wife, Melinda. It broke me that Hope was right. Each of those married couples shared a goal. Gordo and Melinda's shared goal involved their children; that goal explained why he had two nannies and probably explained why he had no issue burning so fast and hard through his severance.

Riley and I had spoken of our goals, of working our asses off to establish a solid savings base before having children, and then reducing our lifestyle once those kids were off to school so we could bankroll even more money to finance a retirement someplace warm in the winter, then travel back north to Chicago (or wherever our children established themselves) in the summer months.

"We had common goals, what happened to them?" I asked, my voice flat and as emotionless as I could manage.

"They died when you disappeared."

"But I'm here now," I reminded her. "I'm never letting go of you, and I swear that no matter what you decide, even when you fly home to Miami, I won't stop fighting for you. You'll see that your idea of common goals still applies to us."

"Our common goal was to meet up one year after college," she reminded me with a sharp edge to her words. "That didn't happen. Nothing you say can change that. We have time, the history of the past, however many years of my searching for you to contend with, Cameron."

I hated that she was so damn right about everything this morning. The ending to this weekend and our happy time together seemed more than just forthcoming, it seemed about as inevitable as breaking a bone or two after jumping off the Sears Tower. The time was lost, and we would never get those seven years back; I couldn't argue about that.

"Maybe it was never a common goal that we had," she said, sighing.

But then I had something, a rebuttal. "Where does delusion play in to this equation, Hope? Because a common goal shared between two people is often the work of a common delusion."

She never missed a beat. She let out a deflated exhale. "Our delusion was that we'd come back, find each other, and pick up where we left off. That we'd be together until the end of time."

She rolled over, and at that moment, as I stared into her hazel eyes full of acceptance and closure, I knew that I had lost her. She had shut me out at some point between last night's freedom and ecstasy and this morning's headache and melancholy.

Do I give up, or do I fight?

"You look lost, Cameron," she said, rolling her fingers along the inside of my forearm. I reveled in the sensation of her touch, wondering why she never admitted—ever—to still loving me.

"I am," I admitted, my throat tight, the words quieter than a whisper. "Here you are, and I feel like you're gone. Like no matter what happened this weekend, no matter what I say now or ever, you're gone."

Still sliding those fingers along my arm, still the tingling of pixie dust in their wake, she came across as extremely calm. I didn't understand it—was it that old fucktart or was she truly done with our love, with me? "You're getting married in a few weeks," she admitted with the emotionless objectivity of a third party.

I chuckled. Partially because she knew what I really wanted here, she knew that I would run away with her. She didn't even have to convince me to back out of my engagement. Yet here she was, ignoring all of that and pushing me back to Riley.

"What do you want me to say, Cameron?" she asked, her face so cold I wanted to believe I was dreaming. Where was Hope from last night? From that night on the wet grass? Why didn't she love me like I loved her?

I felt the air draw from my lungs in one long, depressed breath. I turned away, stepped out of bed, and walked to the chair were I had placed our clothes. "You're not fighting, Hope."

"What should I be fighting for, Cameron?" she asked, tired.

I didn't answer her. Stepping into my pants, I wondered if this sight of her alone on the bed would be my last. This morning had been something of a huge surprise to me as it was…never seeing her again would not have come as much more of a shock.

"I don't believe in fighting for love," she admitted. "You taught me that."

"Then don't fight," I replied, my tone stern enough to let her know I wasn't fucking around. I motioned at my own body. "Don't fight for love, because it's here, right in front of you. This, whatever this is and was over the weekend, is *here*."

She only stared back.

I pointed straight at her to make my position known because the cracking in my voice would definitely not be enough to get the message through to her. "But don't fight for it to go away either. You can't fight one way and not the other, Hope."

She watched me in silence, shaking her head. "What do you want to hear, Cameron?"

I pushed my arms into my shirt with abrupt thrusts. "I want to hear that you will be here in a few hours. That this isn't over, that we're just starting, and that you'll fight as hard as I am."

"Where are you going?" she asked, frowning.

I returned to the bed, kneeling on the mattress to get close enough to Hope so I could kiss the top of her head.

She didn't flinch, didn't look up, but she asked a quiet and quick, "Is this it?"

"You might not want to fight today," I told her, still angry, "but what we have? This doesn't happen in most people's *lifetime*. I'm not letting you go, Hope. I'll fight for this, for *us*, for the rest of my life if I have to."

Refusing to meet my eyes, she lowered her head to the pillow and rolled over. I watched her for a few seconds, watched those shoulders shake as she wept.

"Just be here when I get back," I demanded. And then I left, fearing what faced me back at home, but more determined than ever to make things right with these conflicting promises I had made.

PRESENT DAY

CHAPTER 42

12:13 PM

I find Hope across the street, sitting on a garden ledge at the base of the John Hancock Center. As I approach her, relief floats across my face, and I feel slightly at ease with the fact that she hasn't run back to the office. Or away. Instead, she remains here, sitting and waiting for me.

"Can I sit?" I ask, nodding at the space next to her.

She shrugs, so I sit down and follow her gaze up the crisscrossing surface of the black John Hancock.

"It's beautiful, isn't it?" she says, her voice peaceful. "You see it from the sky, and it looks so flat, almost like glass. But up close, you see all of this iron, and it's pretty but not exactly perfect, is it?"

"What you said at the restaurant—"

"This building is a lot like us, Cameron," she says with a tired sigh. "From the distance, all we remember are those moments of perfection. The fucking, the promises, the so-called love. But up close like this?" She shakes her head. "We're flawed, rusted, and old news."

"You never told me that you love me, not since high

school," I say at last. "Even after everything we've been through. Today at lunch was the first time I heard you admit it. Why would you let it go that long, Hope?" I can feel my heart beating harder at the memory of those words, the impact they had on me. "You talked about wondering for all of those years, wondering what you did wrong…what about me? Even for the past three years, I would've chased you to the end of the world. I still would."

"But you didn't, Cameron. And that makes us flawed," she admits with a tired breath.

I shake my head. The possibility of denial doesn't escape me, but I know what my heart tells me, and it's *not* that we're flawed. It's that we never gave it a chance in the first place. "Why, Hope? What makes us out to be so flawed when we haven't even tried?"

She places her head on my shoulder, and it's a tender gesture despite our talk of being so fucked up. "It's not about trying, it's about existing. And no matter what you say or do, it can't change what has happened between us. Whether it's three years ago, two months ago, or any other time since we walked away from our college promise. You're married, you've cheated on your wife—"

"With you," I point out with a stare of defensiveness. "Always and only you. Because I love you. Yes, more than air, Hope. No matter what you might write in some poem about your beliefs. I've lived half a life, all of those moments without you."

"But I'm the other woman now."

"And I'm always going to be the other man," I counter. "The stakes are even, we're both fucking jerks. Now, can we move on?"

She starts to say something, then closes her mouth, like she's re-thinking her response.

"You always fought so hard to bury those feelings of yours," I tell her. "If you had just let go of trying to fight me off, if you hadn't worked so hard at trying to hate me or forget about me, maybe we could've worked three years ago. Because something tells me that no matter how hard you tried to bury me deep down into your past, I was always present." I let that truth sink in for a beat. "I was always there when you had a moment, when you heard a special word or saw something that reminded you of me. I know it didn't work, Hope, all of that wasted energy on getting rid of me."

She allows a faint grin and shifts her position on the ledge. "You're right," she admits quietly, sounding a little tired. "And it didn't work. It just made me want you more. It made me miss you and ache for you."

I wrap my arm around her and pull her tighter against me, and I wonder if it hurts her neck because her head doesn't leave my shoulder. Feeling her body against mine floods me with memories of our indiscretions since high school, since "moving on." How many times have I been with her, without the fear of losing her?

"Hope," I beg, "you can't move out West. You can't leave me now. We've come this far, and I refuse to let you get on that plane."

"But I am, Cameron. I'm getting on that plane."

"Then I'll follow you," I promise, but the way the words spill out, they sound more like a threat. "I can't exist like this anymore, with these encounters that last a few days or months, and then you're gone. I'd rather follow you and wear you down."

"Isn't that what you're doing today, goob?" she asks, chuckling. At least she doesn't sound hateful or defiant anymore. Like she has accepted my determination and knows she can't stop this—no, she can't stop *us* from happening.

"I'm trying. But I think you're right; I think you'll get on that plane, because that's what you do." But if she thinks I'll let another three years, even another three *days* lapse before we see each other again, she's dead wrong.

At last, she pulls her head off my shoulder and narrows her eyes into annoyed little slits. Maybe she's even more than a little pissed.

I raise my hands in peace, hoping to calm her down. "And I'm fully expecting that you'll go, Hope. I'm fine with that, because I'm coming after you, no matter what you tell me. And I promise that this time, I won't stop. I won't."

Before she can answer, Gordon steps in front of us. He's holding his phone to his face, then says, "I've got him here. Yeah. I'll tell him." He disconnects and asks to speak with me in private. I follow Gordon a few feet away from Hope so we have a bit of privacy. He doesn't look happy; the way his forehead creases when he shoots me with those eyes of his, I know.

"That was Landon," he confesses. "You had some kind of derivatives investment with his firm?"

I reach into my pocket and withdraw my phone. Four more

missed calls. I stuff the phone back in its place. "Japanese Yen."

Gordon closes his eyes and shakes his head.

"I followed his system," I admit with a sigh of defeat. "I needed the cash. It worked with the severance after Harris, and it's how I paid for the condo." My stomach drops at having to admit defeat to the one person who thought better of me. "I took some aggressive positions that only got more and more aggressive as the losses accumulated."

Gordon wipes a hand down his face. "Fuck, Cam. What do you have left?"

I glance back at Hope, mostly to make sure she hasn't left, but also to answer Gordo's question.

He chuckles. "You're kidding, right? Because that won't last long." He checks his Cartier watch. "I'd say that's not going to last more than four more hours."

I give an honest shrug. "It's just money. I made a wrong turn with the Yen, but I'm not making a wrong turn with Hope."

Hope steps into the conversation and elbows me gently. "Is that Newman?" She points across the street to the old water tower. It doesn't take long for me to spot him, licking an ice cream cone for lunch and enjoying the warm, sunny day.

When Gordon spots my boss, he faces me with a huge grin. "The Tesla's still downtown. Where are you two off to now?" He makes an elaborate gesture with his hands, just short of curtsying.

"Fuck off," I say, walking away with my head bowed like Newman won't see me if I do this. "If you had just left me with the car in the first place, none of this would be an issue."

Gordon laughs out loud. Even a moron like Newman would've heard it, but I don't chance a glance back.

CHAPTER 43

12:56 PM

At the Burnham Park Yacht Club, Gordon parks the Tesla next to a Range Rover and groans, "You're fucking kidding me."

I glance over and find Josh speaking to himself inside the expensive SUV; the muffled voice of another man can be heard over the vehicle's speakers, through the slit in the window. Gordon flashes his friend a wave and his executive million-dollar smile, then faces me in the back seat. The smile fades in the heartbeat of an instant.

"You've dragged Josh into this scheme of yours?" he asks.

"Nobody else has a boat like his," I answer. Seems obvious to me.

"We're going out on a boat?" Hope asks from the passenger seat, turning around with a scowl on her face.

I shrug. "It's all part of the plan. You said you'd give me this one day—"

"You're fucking kidding me," Gordon repeats, staring past me out the back window.

When I turn around, I see the catering truck that aroused

Gordon's attention. The caterers retrieve a couple of small containers and head toward the dock entrance. "Oh," I mutter. "That."

Hope lets out a soft chuckle and turns back around, but Gordon's stare remains on me. Like I can read his mind, he shakes his head that this is wrong, but he doesn't have a chance to scold me because Josh has stepped up to Gordon's door and knocks on the window.

Turning around, Gordo opens the window to shake Josh's hand. Josh peeks into the car, and his eyes find me in the back. "You ready, Cam?"

"Been ready for a long time, Josh," I reply, casting a glance at Hope. Yes, a really long time.

He simply nods back, then tells Gordo it's nice to see him. "Are you coming along for the ride?"

I watch Gordon's eyes in the rearview mirror. There's a defiant glint in them all of a sudden and, despite me shaking my head and mouthing *NO!* at him, he smiles and says he would love to.

"We're about half an hour out," Josh says, checking on the marina and activity at the dock. "They're refueling and getting the refreshments ready."

We all step out of the Tesla together. Gordon glances back at me as he slides his arm around Josh's shoulder in the most conspiratorial way imaginable. "We'll catch up, Cam."

I allow a nod, then catch up to Hope as she heads toward the docks where the caterers have just brought a few boxes.

"Great day to be out on the water," I tell her, keeping the

mood light as I ease into the space next to her. "If you leave next week—"

"It's not *if*, it's *when*," she corrects me.

"Okay, then," I agree with an eye roll she can't see. "*When* you leave next week, I want you to have as much of Chicago in your memory as possible. I don't want you to leave without a single thought that doesn't belong to me in some way."

She raises one eyebrow at me. "Why are we here, Cameron? You've got some kind of tension with Gordon, you've got a friend with a boat who's taking us out on the lake, and a boss that will fire you before the end of the day."

I give her a stern, absolute nod. Nothing but the truth. "Three years ago, you showed up out of nowhere and my life changed."

Shaking her head, she responds with an apologetic look. "I'm sorry for that. I was wrong to come for you. I was wrong to let you think we could ever recapture what we had." I wonder if she believes what she said, because I don't.

"I would've lived my life thinking it was all right to split myself in two. One part that was all yours, which I buried. And the other for everything else, so I could drag my ass out of bed and escape in the career I was building. But something I've learned over the past couple months, since running into you, is that's not what life is about, Hope. It's about squeezing every last ounce of happiness from it."

She continues to stare at the big boats. "I'm getting on that plane."

"We only have one shot at this, and it's no secret that I'm getting old here. I'll be thirty next year." I chuckle. "So much of what I want—which is what *we* talked about wanting, when we were together—is slipping away because you're right. I can't escape time; not the years we've let slip by, and not however many years are left for us to live. But I know that if I can't live those years with you, then something's going to have to change. I'm going to have to settle."

"Riley?" she asks.

I stare out at the boats in the harbor. "I don't know; that's her decision to deal with. She deserves better."

"And what about me? Don't I deserve better, Cameron?" Her eyes look pained.

"It's not that geriatric fuck you're with now," I tell her, and I mean it, too. "I know that for sure. And although I believe more than anything else that 'better' is with me, if I'm wrong, then yeah, you deserve better."

She absorbs my words and then steps away from me, walking along the sidewalk that contours the harbor. I follow her, and while she doesn't acknowledge me, I know she senses my presence.

"Maybe you deserve better, too, Cam," she admits with a nonchalance that breaks my heart, no matter how selfless her words might sound. "You definitely don't deserve *this*. None of this nonsense and mind-fucking of the past three years. I hate that I've hurt you, that I've brought you to this, to this point where you think one day with you can overthrow the past five years I've spent with Matt." She shakes her head. "It won't. I'm sorry."

I discover remorse in her face, but I smile with the same confidence that I've always had when it comes to Hope. Because despite the past five years with him, I'm not wrong about what exists between us. I know she came for me three years ago. I know she brushed him off for an entire weekend so she could spend that time with me—just like I brushed off Riley that weekend. I know she came back to my apartment two months ago. I know that she's standing right here in front of me. What I don't know is whether or not she believes the bullshit that just came from her mouth. Even if she does, I know I'm *right* about us; I've always been right. It's why we are here.

"Are you listening to me, Cameron?"

I nod. "I don't care what you say. I let you go once, but it won't happen again. If I'm moving out West to convince you that we belong together, then I'm prepared to do that."

We engage in a staring contest, but I notice Josh and Gordon walking toward us. Time to board the boat, but I have just enough time to hear what's on her mind. I offer her a glimpse of my confidence and determination.

"I won't stop until you're in my arms, Hope."

"You talked about time, Cameron," she says, speaking quickly because she knows Josh and Gordo are getting closer, time is ticking, and we're running out of privacy. "How we've wasted so much and how little of it is left."

"Let's not waste anymore of it," I suggest. "It's as simple as that."

Again with that remorseful expression—her forehead ripples

and her hazel eyes shine with sadness. "You need to walk away from this, otherwise that's what you'll be doing. Wasting your time like I did after high school. And that won't be on my shoulders, okay? It'll be on yours." With that, she crosses her arms and that stare hardens on her face as she locks me out.

Josh and Gordon reach us at last, and I recognize the relief on Hope's face. Like she was saved from me. In many ways, she has been because those last words out of her mouth were fucking harsh and deserving of a response that would soften between now and the time we spoke about this again.

Slapping his hands together, Josh says, "Let's get this party started, shall we?"

THREE YEARS AGO

CHAPTER 44

Stepping through the front door of the townhouse I shared with Riley that Sunday evening after my weekend with Hope, I released a long, deep breath. Within seconds, Riley came hurrying over, the sight of extreme worry flushing her face. She embraced me without getting a response, her body convulsing gently against mine as she wept. When she pulled back, her streaked face and watery eyes begged for answers.

"Where were you?" she asked. There was no confrontation to her tone, just worry.

I opened my mouth to respond, but the words failed to come.

"I was fucking scared something happened to you, Cam," she said, and then hugged me again. "I called Melinda and Gordon, I tried Raj, I even called you!" And then, as if she suddenly remembered the numerous calls I had ignored since Friday, she stepped back again, and the worry morphed into rage. "Where *were* you?"

Stepping away from her, I tried not to think about returning to Hope's hotel room this afternoon, about finding it empty, abandoned.

I had intended on debating whether to come home to Riley and challenging Hope on her depressing view of life. I had my argument all lined up for her, and I had left no room for her to back out. We were supposed to be together. I had planned on staying in that hotel room until she agreed and saw things unfolding no other way.

"I thought we talked about this," I answered at last, shaking the memory of Hope out of my head. "I'm tired. I'm going to bed."

I started climbing the stairs, surprised by how easily I was able to avoid the conversation with Riley, but I heard her footsteps following me. "Talk about *what*, Cam?"

Taking the stairs slowly, I tried to imagine a plausible scenario to tell her. The answer seemed obvious once I reached the second level. "The weekend with Gordo. I'm sure we talked about it."

At the bedroom, I stepped out of my clothes and crawled under the sheets, closing my eyes so Riley would get the point. But she didn't. Instead, she sat on the edge of our bed, on her side. I couldn't see her, but I heard her weeping again.

"Why is she doing this, Cam?" she asked with her broken voice.

I ignored her. Because I no longer knew why Hope was doing this, or who she was anymore, let alone whether I would ever see her again. I couldn't very well answer Riley's question. But she knew. Riley wasn't an idiot, and I could tell she had figured out that my heart—the important part that could love—belonged elsewhere, not with her.

The silence between us stretched so long I feared I had fallen asleep. It made sense. My eyes were closed, and I couldn't remember my thoughts from two seconds ago. Plus, I was so exhausted from making love to Hope all weekend, the idea of a brief, unintentional snooze didn't seem all that far-fetched, even though I figured my heartbreak wouldn't allow any rest at all. When I heard Riley get up and walk away, I realized that as much as I wished I had been sleeping, I hadn't.

Before walking out of the room, Riley turned around at the doorway. "Open your eyes, Cam."

I opened them. I hated seeing her upset—the messed up makeup, the streaks down her face.

"I don't care what you did," she declared, sniffling and wiping her sleeve across her suddenly determined and strong face. "I don't care where you were. I just want to know. I want to know what I'm up against here, because this thing of ours? For the past few weeks or months, it's not been the happy place it once was. It's been hell, and I want it to end."

I didn't spend too much time watching her. I simply rolled over, curled my legs up toward my chest, and wondered why Hope had disappeared without saying her final goodbye.

CHAPTER 45

Thursday morning, the doorbell rang. From my desk in the second bedroom, I heard Riley open the door and carry on a muffled conversation before shouting upstairs at me that it was Gordon. I hadn't heard from him all week, and his absence had been something of a break for me, allowing me to wallow in my state of depression and agree to an interview with Raj and some middle-management types who would underpay and over-abuse me at a small financial services firm known as Second City Financial.

"Get dressed!" Gordo yelled upstairs.

I saved my resume, then showered and donned a pair of jeans with a black collared shirt. When I hurried downstairs, I saw that Riley had invited Gordon into the house and poured him a cup of coffee while he waited for me. She kept him company, packing herself a light lunch and getting last night's dishes loaded into the dishwasher.

When I appeared downstairs, Gordon seemed to do a double-take, but he hid the surprise at seeing me. I had possibly lost a few pounds. My pants were loose around my waist, and my shirt was a little baggier than normal.

"All set?" he asked from the table.

"Yeah," I said, shrugging. "What are we up to?"

He chuckled, shaking his head. "Miami and then Nassau overnight."

Riley smiled from the counter, all set to leave for work. "Sounds like fun." Then to me specifically, she raised an inquiring eyebrow and asked, "When will you have time to find a job with all of this fun stuff, Cam?"

Gordon stood. Trying to lighten the mood, he wrapped his arms around Riley. Maybe a little longer than he should've, but I knew how much he liked her. "I've got half a dozen friends who will make sure he's employed before the end of next week."

"I hope so," Riley said, wiggling free and walking to the front foyer. The way she said *hope* felt like a shaving cut. "Cam doesn't manage his time very well when he's home with nothing to do."

"I'll take care of him and have him back to you tomorrow night," Gordo promised, joining her at the foyer. "He's yours all weekend."

She pulled her shoes on, bending over with her ass facing the door, which seemed to disappoint Gordo a little. I shook my head and started back toward the eat-in dining area when Riley asked, "Speaking of weekends, did you have fun last weekend with Cam?"

The question stopped me in my tracks, but thanks to the wall between the kitchen and foyer, Riley would never know. Gordo backed up enough to make eye contact with me, and his eyes had question marks in them. He consulted Riley again, then stared back at me.

Don't fuck me now, Gordo, I thought, my face burning up with the fear that he would do exactly that.

The sadistic little smirk rose up on his lips as he studied me, further intensifying the heat in my face and the fear in my chest.

"Cam," he said, with a light-hearted chuckle that only his closest friends—AKA, me—would recognize as fake. "Didn't you tell Riley about the blast we had?" Then, to Riley, "They say some weekends are made for building memories, but last weekend was a memory of a lifetime." He chuckled again. "I wouldn't trade it for the world, Riley. If it had been appropriate to have you along, you'd know exactly what I'm talking about."

I thought I might piss my pants, but I held myself together as Riley peeked around the corner and blew me a kiss. "Have a nice time away, Cam. Remember to keep your phone on."

As she left the house, Gordon called after her, "Where's *my* kiss?" He forced his executive-salesman laugh and closed the door once she was gone. What a fucking gentleman.

I stood in that wasted space between the foyer and the kitchen/eat-in dining area, wondering if I would truly know whether I had just emptied my bladder into my pants. My entire body felt numb. Would the warmth of urine trickling down my leg be noticeable?

I thanked Gordo once he returned to the table for his coffee, then walked to the refrigerator for a cold bottled water. I needed it to cool my body panicked body temperature down, wash the heat off my face, and rehydrate my system after that sudden onslaught of sweating-my-balls-off. Fuck, that was a close call.

From behind me, Gordon cleared his throat. "What

happened last weekend, Cam?"

I suspected he knew, but I lied to him anyway. "Pre-wedding jitters. Needed a bit of time to myself, that's all." I closed the refrigerator door, my mind already racing toward Miami and the possibilities. "Are we ready to go?"

Gordon finished his coffee in a final sip, rinsed it in the sink, and then placed it in the dishwasher, which Riley hadn't started. Despite being a huge pain in the ass, with more money than real-life street smarts, Gordo was a decent guy. No wonder Riley liked him and trusted me to spend so much time with him.

"We'll talk about last weekend," he warned me as we left my townhouse and settled into his Tesla. "It better not be what I think it is."

CHAPTER 46

Except we didn't get to talk about last weekend. Once we arrived at the airport and boarded the Cessna that Landon had a timeshare-like interest in, Gordon was easily lost in the conversations about the markets, the technical analysis of grain prices combined with Asian demand trends, and a bunch of other things that numbed my ears. So while Gordon and a senior strategist from Landon's company spoke about these things, I closed my eyes.

Until Landon dropped into the seat next to me, which was a little awkward because there were plenty of other seats available on the jet. I glanced up at Josh, who was reading the newspaper in the rear-facing seat across from me. The glance he gave me justified my curiosity in Landon's sudden seating change.

"Hey, Cam," Landon said, keeping his voice low. "Want a blow job?"

I nearly jumped, which made the flamboyant trader laugh so loud, even the pilot turned around to cast us a questioning glance.

"Just fucking with your head, Cam." He patted my leg and wiggled his eyebrows at me to pique my interest. "I made two-point-five million last year. I don't know if Gordon shared that with you, since I ask him to keep that shit to himself, but you never know."

I shook my head and swallowed hard because I was a little nervous about where this was headed after the blowjob comment. "No, he never mentioned it."

"Well, it doesn't matter because I'm telling you anyway. But this isn't a conversation about how big my dick is." He shoots me a cocky wink. "This is a conversation about how I can help you out."

"With my dick size or my unemployment earnings?" I smirked sideways, impressed with my wit given how nervous he made me.

Landon thought that was funny, and the pilot glanced back at him yet again. "I know you're sitting on a bit of cash, Cam. What if I could turn your Harris severance into a million dollars? Would that make you hard?"

I couldn't help but shift a little in my seat. With a million dollars, I could do a lot of things. Including avoid employment while I fixed my head and heart after Hope disappeared on me. Yet, somehow, images of Bernie Madoff and his wild and crazy Ponzi schemes floated through my thoughts.

Landon reached into his pocket for a business card. "I'll show you how I do it. It's high-risk derivatives stuff, but it's how I got started in college." He shrugged again like it was no big deal. "Gordon says you're a smart guy, but you're way over-qualified for what we need. If you take what I teach you and make a go at it, maybe you can start trading." He patted my leg before standing up. "Think about it, Cam. It's a lot of money."

He returned to his seat, and I couldn't help but stare out the window at the clouds beneath the wings. Not that I expected to find answers there, but they offered no hints as to what I should do with Landon's invitation to turn my severance into a million dollars. I wondered at the risk—he *had* mentioned there would be some risk involved. And then I started planning on how I could survive off a million dollars while convincing Hope to run away with me.

These daydreams of a life I couldn't imagine for myself led me to my iPhone. And a Google search for Hope McManus in Miami. I found half a dozen addresses before finally tapping the one link I had wanted to avoid entirely: Facebook. I scrolled through the photos, taking note of the landmarks in the background, ignoring the big smiles she shared with that dickhead she had been eating lunch with last week.

And then I had my answer—a pic of a two-seater Mercedes convertible, the SLK, in the driveway of her house. Alone, the pic meant nothing outside of the fact that Hope drove an amazing vehicle and lived on an expensive suburban street. In the background, however, I found a street sign. Once I zoomed in on that street sign, I knew where she lived because I recognized the name from the White Pages directory.

I didn't realize it right away, but tracking her down had made me happy enough that I discovered an imposter's smile on my face. Across from me, Josh watched with a foreign interest. But when I raised my attention to him, he glanced back to the newspaper. Although I wanted to pat myself on the back with a cheer for this minor victory, I stayed quiet, rested my head back, and closed my eyes. I plotted the next few hours in my head, everything from getting out of

Nassau to lining up a rental car in Miami, Hope's hometown. And how, before sunset, I would be standing outside the house that I located on my phone.

For now, I needed to concentrate on and script what I planned to say to her.

CHAPTER 47

The marina, where Landon had rented a race-worthy Donzi, had an attached hotel. We checked into a suite, using Landon's credit card, and had lunch brought up. I didn't eat much, so when the call from the concierge arrived that the boat was ready for us, nobody challenged me when I told them I didn't feel so hot. Well, Josh and Landon had no issue. Gordo seemed skeptical.

While the others changed into their fancy swim trunks, shirts, and donned sunscreen, Gordo approached me, keeping his voice low as he asked me if my sudden illness had anything to do with last weekend.

I faked a surprised look. "Not at all, Gordo. I was in Chicago the entire time, and I'm feeling a lot better now."

He hemmed and hawed.

"I'll be here the entire time," I lied. I would have told him I'd be performing open-heart surgery if it meant getting him and the others out of here. "Call whenever you want."

Landon called after Gordon to hurry up. They were ready to leave.

At last, Gordon patted my back and said he hoped I felt

better. "I'll see you tomorrow afternoon when we get back, and then we'll talk about last weekend."

"Looking forward to it," I said, and this time I meant it because between now and then, I'd have Hope in my arms, and nothing he could say would matter.

Once the guys left, I stepped out to the balcony and watched them below as they headed through the secure gates to the dock. Someone else greeted them and brought them on board to explain the vessel. The owner instructed Josh, who was arguably the most familiar with navigating the seas. Within half an hour, the engines were rumbling and Josh guided the boat out of the marina.

Returning to the room, I called the front desk and asked about obtaining a rental car.

"Give us thirty minutes," the concierge promised.

I retreated to the bathroom, showered, and fixed myself up. I had definitely lost a bit of weight since last weekend; I could see it in my reflection. My stomach looked flatter, gaunter with such a thin layer of skin that my abdominal muscles began to stretch through, and I could see a cleaner jaw line in my face. Although I wasn't unrecognizable, I figured Hope would notice the slight difference, just as Gordo had.

In the hotel lobby, I saw they had set aside a Mustang convertible for me.

"Will this be charged to the credit card we hold for the room?" the concierge asked.

Grinning, I confirmed that it would, and then grabbed the

keys. After programming Hope's address into the GPS, I set off. Forty minutes later, I was parked across the street from her house. I spotted the FOR SALE sign immediately and wondered why they were selling. The Mercedes from her Facebook picture was the only car in the driveway. The garage door was also wide open, and I saw that there was no other vehicle parked inside.

Hope was home. Alone.

I considered getting out of the car and walking to the front door, but some kind of fear held me back. Was it the rejection from this past weekend that haunted me? Was that causing this sudden bout of gun-shyness? I pounded the steering, sitting in this open-roofed Mustang, across the street from Hope's house.

Without question, I looked like an idiot.

Then I felt her. I stopped abusing the rental car and stared back across the street at Hope's house, and there she stood outside her front door. She wore tight jogging shorts and a form-fitting running top.

Her eyes were locked on me.

I could barely breathe her name.

Slowly and carefully, I opened the car door and stepped out onto the road without looking. I didn't dare avert my eyes for fear that Hope might start running. And as much as I had enjoyed tackling her outside of the community center in the rain, I really didn't want to be tackling her in this neighborhood. Plus, I wouldn't be able to compete with the high-end Asics she wore.

Raising my empty hands to show how defenseless I was, I

crossed the street and stepped across her front lawn to the front porch. There were two steps and roughly four feet separating us.

"Hope," I said, a little breathless thanks to the nerves.

"Cameron." Her hazel eyes seemed distrustful, surprised and relieved, all at once.

And then we had one of our famous staring contests.

She blinked first.

"Why?" I asked, and the hurt spilled out of my mouth.

Her chin quivered. "You," was her answer, and I didn't know what that meant, but I erased the distance between us with two leaping steps and kissed her. Hard.

She hooked an arm around my neck and fumbled for the door, twisting the knob after several attempts, and then she kicked it open; the wall stopped it with a *thud,* and we hurried inside, in case the neighbors were watching.

In the foyer, I tried to force her up against the door once I closed it, but she twirled around and shoved me against the door. She was strong, and the force kicked the wind out of my lungs.

I didn't care, though. I wanted her. I needed to have her, now.

"I missed you," I said between breaths, but she was pulling her tight top over her head and kissing me before she could utter a response.

I felt her hands working at the belt of my pants, slowly stripping me in the foyer of her house. Stepping out of the pants, I massaged her breasts as she guided me backward into the vast kitchen.

I trusted her directions, even though she moved her lips and tongue over my mouth, neck, and chest blindly, hungrily.

The kitchen island forced my backward stumble to a blunt stop, and Hope's lips worked their magic below the waistband of my boxers. As she ran her tongue along my rigid shaft, the world spun, and I reached down, gripping her hair and tugging her face to mine. We kissed hard, my fingers reaching between down low. She spread her legs, opened them to provide me with greater access to her clit. I massaged her in a soft, circular motion, then dipped my middle finger inside her to see just how wet she was.

"Cameron," she moaned quietly.

Her voice transformed me from a quiet bystander to an active hunter. Reaching down to her waist, I lifted her off the floor, spun around, and planted her on the kitchen island. Either the cold granite annoyed her, or she liked that I was taking control. Either way, Hope pulled my face to hers and kissed me with a ravenous hunger.

"I love you," I whispered, pulling her hips to the edge of the island and rubbing the head of my cock along her pussy. And just then, she reached behind her for the exhaust vent, holding herself up and angling her hips in such a way that I entered her easily, slowly, gently at first, but at the first sound of her moaning "Oh, Cameron!" I thrust a little deeper, a little harder, and a little faster.

She moaned a little louder, and I didn't last long. Watching the woman I loved enjoy what I was doing to her on the kitchen island made me want her more and more.

When I was about to pull out, Hope said, "No," and then

wrapped her legs around my waist, locking me in place so I had no choice but come inside her, in sync with her own pulsating orgasm.

By the time our bodies cooled off, she released the vent and rested back on her elbows, her dreamy eyes staring at mine. We didn't speak for a long time, but the hunger was unmistakable. She wiped at the sweat beading on her forehead.

"What are you doing here?" I asked, looking around the nice house. It was just as I imagined her house would be when I was in high school—cold without much personality, sterile but still homely enough to double as a model home.

Hope laughed. "Shouldn't I be the one to ask that question?"

I told her that I had been "dragged" along by Gordon, an old colleague who had received a severance package on the same day as me. "Once I found out that he was coming to Miami, and I remembered that you said you would be back yesterday…I had to try, Hope." I shook my head, a little embarrassed but also incredibly proud that I hadn't "stopped" this time. I had fought for her, fought for her love, something she had never believed in. "I haven't been sleeping or eating or breathing since I returned to your hotel Sunday afternoon and found that you'd left." Speaking with her about this stuff while naked at her kitchen island seemed strangely therapeutic. I didn't feel so sad now. Still, I had to know. "Why did you leave like that? You didn't even say goodbye…" Because *goodbyes are forever*, I realized.

My question forced her to look elsewhere to avoid whatever guilt she felt. "I couldn't see you again, Cameron."

I reached down and started to pull my boxers up. "But you

could've left without seeing me again? Without saying…goodbye?" She had known it would not be forever, that we would see each other again. Maybe not this soon, but still…

She rolled off the island and grabbed her workout gear, which was scattered in a path from the front door to the kitchen. "I'm afraid of goodbyes, you know that. The last time I watched you leave, I didn't see you again for seven years." She shook her head at me, her hands full as she walked past me toward a hallway. "I didn't say goodbye this time, and now look, you're in my kitchen, in Miami."

I followed her into the hall, to a bedroom at the end. "Yes, I came for you. I've admitted that I was wrong to do what I did, so now what?" I asked.

"Now I get changed and follow you to your hotel, or somewhere else, anywhere else, because Matt will be home in half an hour." She gave a look that promised we could talk all about this stuff later.

I reached out, grabbed her wrist, and pulled her against me. "Leave him," I pleaded. "Come back with me, and let's do this together."

She seemed to consider my suggestion, but I could see she didn't place a whole lot of weight in it. At last, she shook her head, pulled free, and headed to the walk-in closet to pack a bag. "How long are you in Miami?"

"Just overnight," I said, groaning.

She peeked out of the closet. "Exactly."

Confused, I joined her in the closet, a room with fancy wooden panels, an ironing board, mannequin-like hangers, a television, steamer, enclosed shoe wardrobe, pretty much a dry-cleaner's wet dream.

"You have a really nice place, Hope. But what did you mean by 'exactly'?"

"You're here overnight, Cameron," she explained. "That's what I meant by 'exactly.'"

"What the fuck does that mean?" I asked, a little annoyed.

She shoved a few more items into her bag. "You don't want me to say goodbye, you want me to drop my entire life here and run off with someone who's in Miami 'overnight'?" She chuckled and shook her head at me. "I know how stories like this turn out, Cameron."

I leaned against the staging table. She stepped up to the other side and leaned against that end. We were facing off in her walk-in closet that seemed straight out of Oz.

"Tell me, Hope," I encouraged her. "Please. How do these stories turn out?"

A confrontational frown wafted across her face, and she tapped the edge of the staging area with her fingers. "Did you read that email a few weeks ago? The story?"

I nodded. "It's not us, Hope. We're not these two characters. You leave that old fucktart you're living with, and I'll walk away from Riley. I swear—"

She cut me off. "You won't."

"I will," I promised, throwing my arms into the air before reaching out for her, but she stopped me. Shaking her head, she gave me a sideways glance.

"Uh-uh, no way. You've got a wedding in three weeks, Cameron. You have a future and a past. Both of which are filled with memories of which you won't ever let go. And do you think, for one second, that I'm sitting here and believing that you'll abandon all of that history? For me? For a girl you fucked in high school?"

I breathed heavily, afraid to respond because she had a bit of a point.

She gave a sly wink. "I *know* how this turns out for us."

"I will let go, Hope." I drop to a knee.

"I know you will. Now get up, goob."

"Not you, though. I'm never letting go of you again."

She bit down on her lower lip. I could almost hear the gears turning in her head as she contemplated my big-man talk. At last, she tapped the top of the staging area and stood straight. Conversation over.

"If you want to spend the night with me, we need to leave." She grabbed her bag and started to leave, but turned back at the door. "Now, Cameron. Matt will be home, and I guarantee you don't want to be around when he shows up. Not after last weekend."

PRESENT DAY

CHAPTER 48

2:18 PM

Out on the Lake Michigan with the sun beating down on us, I stare across the small table at Hope. Behind her, I only see the emptiness of the lake meeting up with the promising sky on the horizon. Behind me, the Chicago skyline looms, and I know Hope likes that view because it's something I would enjoy. I see the city's reflection in her big sunglasses, the ones that hide her face and lend her an air of confidence. She picks up her champagne flute and takes a sip before reaching into a small bowl of fresh fruit that the catering company provided.

Up on the captain's deck, slightly up and behind me, Gordon sits with his chair rotated so that he can chaperone us. When I glance over at him, I find a distrustful semi-smile on his face. We share a brief stare before he points his two fingers at his eyes, then aims those fingers at me, the international sign for *I'm watching you.* Almost like a threat.

"It's not Miami," I admit, turning my attention back to Hope. "But I never wanted this to be Miami. I only ever wanted this to be *us.*"

"Cameron," she sighs, "I don't know what you really thought today would achieve, but—"

"But nothing," I argued. "What have you thought about today? So far?"

She shrugs, but a smile slips onto her face. She doesn't fight it away, either. She lets it live, and I see that as a sign of promise.

"For me," I tell her, feeling the history between us, "today reminded me of something that I seemed to have lost track of."

Her eyebrows raise halfway up her forehead. "And what was that? Your GPS?" She laughs at her own weak joke.

I feel something hit me in the shoulder and glance back to find Gordo flinging grapes at me.

"Let it go, Cameron," he says, chuckling. "Today will *not* turn out like you want." He nods at Hope. "I think everyone's on the same page here. Everyone but you."

I face Hope again, determined. He was worth the distraction. "I've decided that I'm never letting go again. I've chased you across this godforsaken country. I've sacrificed everything. Everything I've ever done, somehow and some way, was because of you."

She removes her sunglasses so I can see her clear, unflinching eyes. "There's something romantic about goodbyes, Cameron. Even though I've never been able to bring myself to say that one word to you, if nothing else, today has made it clear that I need to set my personal rules and superstitions about goodbyes aside. Because this isn't fair to you. You've put your life on hold because of me, and it's not supposed to be like that."

I glance back at Gordo on the captain's deck, but he has turned his back to me, to my conversation. Intuitive as always, he must've detected the heavy tone in our conversation and decided to give us a bit of privacy at last.

"I'm sorry, Cameron," she says, her voice soft. When I turn back to her, the sunglasses have been pulled back over her eyes, hiding them once again. Her granite-like face tells me something isn't quite right. Or maybe, I realize for the first time since this delusion of a day began, *everything* is right, and I'm only seeing that for the first time, right now.

"Let me paint a picture for you," I say, keeping my voice quiet and leaning in to get a little closer. "I'm not quitting you. It's not that I don't want to, Hope. It's that I can't. I simply cannot walk away from you." I lean back in my chair, reclining as best as I can and trying to hide the nervous sweat threatening to soak through my armpits. "After you showed up three years ago, I realized something. You can't bury people alive. And that's what I tried to do through college and in the years that followed. I was trying to bury you because I didn't want to admit to myself that I could never exist without you. I couldn't handle it. And ever since that day? You've consumed my thoughts. My dreams. My every breathing moment."

I watch her face for what feels like an eternity, and then I see it. A small twitch at the corner of her lips.

"Cameron..." she says with a tone of disappointment, but instead of finishing her thought, she lets my name linger.

I shake my head. "You showed up for a reason. And you win.

You were right. Whatever you were trying to prove, you were right, Hope."

She wipes at her face, the first sign of emotion.

"You were right," I tell her again, even softer.

"Cameron, I'm not looking for 'right,'" she admits, a little frustrated despite the previous show of emotion. "I'm looking for you to let me go, to say the word that I've never been able to say. That's what you promised, remember? If I spent the day with you, you said this morning in that doorway, you promised you'd let me go, you'd say goodbye."

A sailboat moves across the background, so I watch it to add a little silence to our conversation. "I'm not looking for right either."

"Then what are you looking for?"

I give her a half-shrug. "I'm looking for happy. I'm looking for the smiles you've given me every day I've seen you, every morning when I wake up thinking that I'll possibly see you, take you in, admire you. I'm looking for you in everything I do. Just you, and nothing else."

Her silence speaks more than any words she could give me. She's thinking about it. Again, I feel those wheels of hers turning. I can feel her eyes on me through those tinted, large sunglasses, and for a second, I want to take a deep breath and try to read her mind because it seems to me that I can do exactly that.

"Hope, it's always been you."

"Cameron…"

"Okay, okay," I say, raising my hands in a peace offering. "It's not 'just you.'"

"Gee, thanks."

"It's you when you're with me." I smile, but she doesn't return the gesture. "What? I thought that was sweet. Why are you such a downer?"

"It was sweet," she admits, picking at her fingernails. "It's one of the sweetest things anyone has ever said to me. But that's the problem with this, Cameron. This sweetness? The way you love me. I mean, the way you love me so perfectly?" She shakes her head. "It can't happen, it can't be. I'm sorry. I'm so very sorry, but you and I…?"

I take my champagne to hide my disappointment, noticing how I have a little more than half the flute left to drink. Although it's probably warmer than piss by now, I swallow it in a single gulp, the bubbles burning the back of my throat. "If you get on the plane next week," I tell her, my eyes digging through those big glasses, "I'll be right behind you."

She shakes her head. "You can't. That's not part of this deal."

I quietly argue, "He can't come close to offering you what I can."

"It'll be goodbye, one way or another," she mutters, almost sadly.

I contemplate what to say next. I know I can't sit back and watch her get on that plane, but I also know that, once the day is over, she will not come to me. The reality of that rips me apart because I was so convinced, earlier today, that she would say those four words—I'm leaving you—before the day ends. But now I know; goodbye will come, and Hope believes that goodbyes are forever.

I take a deep breath. "Even if we never see each other again," I admit as calmly as my raging disappointment will allow, "you're in this as deep as I am, Hope. It's inescapable."

She looks around like she's planning a getaway, some way to avoid this conversation, some exit to this corner that I have backed her in to. Of course, she finds no escape, and the realization that she's stuck here, on this boat in the middle of Lake Michigan with nothing but water around us, slowly settles over her. I don't know if there is peace or fear behind those big glasses, but she eventually succumbs and listens to me, to what I say.

"After what happened three years ago, I beat myself up for following you to Miami, because I would've gone with you wherever you wanted me to. I would've followed you to the edge of the universe, Hope. But it killed to leave you, it killed me to see you walk away with him."

"Cameron, why are we talking about this?" she asks, but I ignore her.

"And with time, I dealt with that sadness. I dealt with it because I knew that I wasn't suffering alone. I gave you the space you needed to come back for me."

She shakes her head. "I never came back for you."

I raise my eyebrows at her obvious denial. "But you did."

She crosses her arms.

"And even if you hadn't, we were still together. In spirit. In love. The silence between us killed me, it fucking ripped me apart,

Hope. But I knew when you missed me, when that absence burned you up inside. And I knew when you forgot about me for a day or two." I close my eyes and take an elaborate breath, inhaling my courage and letting it all out through my lips, yoga-style. With my eyes clamped shut, I tell her, "We're connected, somehow and some way, I don't know how or why, but we are."

When I open my eyes, I find her staring back just like I left her before I closed my eyes.

"That's the tragedy here," I ramble on. "We both suffer, whether we're together in each other's arms, or we're separated by thousands of miles."

I feel more grapes on my shoulder, but I refuse to take my eyes from her. I'm watching for that one sign. Some kind of acknowledgement that I've hit a nerve, or fear that I've completely lost my mind.

At last, Hope speaks, but it's not for me. "Gordon, will you just fuck off for a minute?"

Gordo chuckles, but I detect his annoyance with Hope. He never liked her, always a Team Riley proponent. "Are you two ready to head back so you can return to your respective spouses?"

I watch Hope, but she remains firmly focused on me. So I nod an affirmative.

The boat's deep, rumbling engines come to life, and the ripe aroma of gasoline infiltrates the air out here.

Hope shakes her head at me. "Cameron, I never wrote any that stuff in *Our Story*. None of it. It's not us because Emma knows nothing about us."

I don't believe her. And as much as I want to continue with this conversation, any kind of exchange between us becomes impossible thanks to the sounds of the boat as it cut across the lake, back toward to the city.

THREE YEARS AGO

CHAPTER 49

Late Friday morning, leaving the hotel with Hope's hand locked in mine, I noticed Gordon and the other guys returning. The shadows underneath their eyes told some of the story of their fun in Nassau overnight, but the fatigue and whatever other pains they were dealing with did nothing to deter Gordon from spotting us and heading straight for us. I released her hand and stepped away, something that clearly annoyed her.

"Hey, Gordo—" I started, but he cut me off, extending a hand to Hope and introducing himself.

"And you must be Hope," he said as they shook hands. "I've heard so much about you." He shifted his attention to me, but only briefly enough for me to recognize his rage.

"I've heard about you, as well," Hope said. "I see unemployment has been good to you."

"Did Cam invite you to his wedding in a few weeks?" Gordon asked her, feigning confusion as he directed his next question at me. "Or do you think Riley would take exception to high school whores showing up out of the blue?"

"Gordo—" I started between my clenched teeth, but Hope

was not one to back down.

She shifted her body sideways, scowling at me before facing Gordon dead-on. "It will be interesting to see if Cam himself shows up to that wedding, let alone whether the so-called 'whore' shows up."

I watched Gordo open his mouth to spew what would likely be the most childish rebuttal ever, but then he seemed to think better of it and asked me, "Are you having second thoughts about next month?"

"Not just me," I confessed, "but Riley, too."

He gave a rude sideways nod to Hope. "All because of this one?"

I shook my head at him, mostly pissed off. "It's complicated, Gordo…"

Hope stepped forward and took his hand. "Actually, it's not complicated. Cam and I made a promise."

"Hope," I started, but Gordo cut me off.

"So I've heard, some fucking promise."

Hope withdrew her hand, splitting her attention between Gordo and me. "We will always have that broken promise. Whether he gets married to some distraction for five minutes or fifty years, what we have is boundless, it's never constrained. Even time itself couldn't keep us apart."

"Wow, that's super deep," I said, breathless and meaning it.

Gordon smirked. He nodded. He rolled his hand down the length of his face. And then something else caught his attention, his focus drifting past me at a man seated in one of the lobby chairs. He wore a hat, but there was no question—this was the same douche who had been eating lunch on the terrace with Hope last week.

The geriatric fuck stood and started marching toward us once he realized that we had all seen him and were aware of his presence in the lobby. None of us flinched, not even Hope. She remained at my side.

"Fuck, it's Matt," she whispered, her voice tight with anticipation. "This won't be a happy moment."

In the time it took him to take those dozen or so footsteps to reach me, I reminded myself of the few facts I knew about this grandpa. First, he was an accountant, and without his calculator the only weapon he had was, well, nothing. Second, he was older than Hope, obviously in his forties, so stamina and strength were *not* on his side. Third, Hope had just had a second consecutive weekend fucking me, so I obviously owned her, and he was the idiot whose lease was about to expire.

Advantage: me.

"What's going on here?" he asked, his voice stern and his face red with the kind of rage that sits a mere hair's width between you and a prison term. "Hope? Is this the guy?"

I extended my hand, grinning. "Yes, I'm the one who is more her age."

He didn't like that. He smacked my hand away, which got Gordo excited, as well as Josh and Landon and the other guy whose name I failed to remember at that moment. The four of them stepped forward. The hotel staff was also noticing the tension here, and I trusted that someone had picked up the phone to call for reinforcements.

"I don't fucking care if you're the tooth fairy," he growled at me. "You're seven years too late, dickhead."

"Interesting," I blurted, fully aware that my arrogance had turned off my internal filter or ability to think, "that's not what your kitchen counter would say."

Matt took a swing at me, but Gordon lunged forward and gave him a shove, throwing him off balance and causing his balled fist to hit Gordo in the shoulder instead. No harm. Yet.

"Cam, shut the fuck up," Gordo warned me. Then to the old guy, "Get your whore of a wife out of here before someone gets beaten." He tried to shove Hope away, but she slapped his hand back.

Matt removed his hat and wiped the sleeve of his shirt along his forehead. He was clearly pissed. "If I see you near Hope again…" he threatened.

"Be thankful," I said, squaring my shoulders and wondering why the fuck Hope wasn't next to me, "it's not like we fucked in your bed. And being a bean counter, you'll be happy that she won't be looking for you to invest in many more of those blue pills—"

That time, *Gordo* swung at me. And he connected. I tasted blood before I realized he hit me, and it knocked me over. A few patrons in the hotel lobby gasped. *Fucker.* When I regained my bearings, I was a little dizzy, but I could still see the smirk on Matt's face as he took Hope's arm and steered her away. He maintained his satisfied grin for a couple of paces before he bore down on the hotel entrance.

"See you around," I said, the bitterness so thick I spit it onto the carpet in the form of blood. Then, to Gordo, I added, "You're a dickhead."

Gordo shook his head, his eyes wide with shock. Probably at my temporary moment of insanity. "You're lucky he didn't kill you."

"Fuck you," I snapped, shoving through my entourage and heading toward the elevators.

But Gordo was convinced he had just performed an incredible act of valor. He ran to catch up to me, grabbing my elbow. "He had a gun, asshole." He brought his lips closer to my ear. "Didn't you see it, or were you too fucking blind from that bullshit promise?"

I didn't care if Matt had come with a bomb. All I wanted was Hope, and now she was gone.

The elevator doors opened, and all five of us stepped on board. Nobody else said anything, not even to try and lighten the mood. It was during our ascent that I realized something that I should've picked up a few seconds prior. And it burned. A lot.

Hope hadn't even looked back at me, hadn't stood up for herself. She had left willingly with that asshole, and that was one message I couldn't ignore—she had chosen him.

Not me.

CHAPTER 50

I opened my eyes at two AM for no reason, waking up completely. I stared up at the ceiling with nothing but the pale moonlight providing a soft, romantic illumination that made the white sheets glow. Glancing over at Riley, I watched her sleep, her mouth slightly open, her eyes as peaceful as I'd ever seen them since Hope had come back and turned our plans upside down. I reached out and stroked her hand, which was lodged underneath her pillow. A smile surfaced, and her hand edged out enough that I could hold it in mine.

Returning my attention to the ceiling, I wondered why I was suddenly alert so early. The only thing I could think was that Hope had somehow infiltrated my dreams and pushed the memory of her and our love back into consciousness. Like she could actually do that.

Riley retracted her hand and rolled over so all I could see was her narrow back, and I decided to relieve myself. I wondered how many times Hope's geriatric fiancé awoke during the night to take a piss. Was this my future?

After I washed my hands, I wondered about going back to bed. Rather than tossing and turning and disrupting Riley's sleep, I tiptoed to the second bedroom where I had left my laptop earlier. I was suddenly curious about that novel Hope had sent me. But when I accessed my email account, I saw that she had sent me another message.

Ten minutes ago.

Frowning, I wondered if she truly *had* woken me somehow so that I could make a trip to my computer and find this little "gift" from her. Spooky.

I ignored her message, though, and went straight to the one with the attachment. Convinced that I needed to ignore Hope if I wanted to lead a happier, saner life with Riley, it wasn't hard to pretend this early morning message didn't exist in the first place. After all, I wanted to read the novel, not another mind-fuck of an email.

Our Story.

The novel.

Right.

I had read a good chunk of *Our Story*, probably two chapters or so when she first sent it, but now I wanted to read the whole thing, find out more about this love story between Oliver and Olivia, and what it could mean for Hope when she insisted it was written by Emma Payne.

So I opened the attachment and read it.

Again.

And again.

By the time I finished with the novel, which was more like a novella because it was so short (one hundred and eighteen pages sure sounded longer than the story suggested), I had tears in my eyes and a throat that felt so tight I could barely breathe.

"Are you okay?"

I spun around in my chair and found Riley standing in the doorway, her housecoat hanging open to reveal her white, lacey panties, her flat, soft tummy. I loved circling my tongue around her navel and kissing a path a little farther south.

"Cam?" she asked, her flirty tone teasing me from the doorway. "Are you okay?"

She stepped toward me. A week ago, I would've hidden the screen, but not tonight. Once she reached me, she slipped one hand through my hair and used the other to tilt the laptop screen so that she could read the words on the screen.

"What are you reading?"

I shrugged, shaking my head just enough that her fingers slipped out of my hair and traced a path down along my face, slowly. She lowered herself into my lap, adjusted the screen again.

"It's called *Our Story*?" she asked. She looked at me again, the curiosity twisting her lips. "I like it," she admitted. She could not have read more than a paragraph. "Can I read it?"

"You sure? Hope sent it."

She tilted her head to the side, as if measuring me, my words. "Do you love me, Cam?"

"Of course I do." I wrapped my arms around her waist and gave her a subtle squeeze. "I'm here."

She kissed my lips with the tenderness of our past, pre-Hope life, then pulled back, angling her chin down and staring at me with pouty eyes. "Then let me read it."

"You won't like it. It's about two married people who fall in love and end up together."

She scrolled through a few pages, stopping for a bit to read. "Did Hope write this for you?"

My eyes rolled across the words on the screen.

He raised his glass as if in a toast. At first, I thought he might be dismissing what I had just said. "Sometimes, love brings us into the darkest corners of our lives," he told me. "But we survive because love guides us through the fears and uncertainties. And other times, love brings us into the brightest sunshine, the most absolute happiness we will ever know."

I remembered that excerpt from an earlier chapter. It seemed appropriate that Riley would scroll to this specific part of the novel. Olivia and Oliver were aboard a yacht of some sort in Miami. It seemed bizarre because I had just come from Hope's house in Miami.

"She says she didn't," I admitted, shrugging. "But…I don't know if I believe her."

Riley nodded, scrolling down a little more but didn't spend any time reading the next area where she stopped. "Well, if I want any part of your future, I think I should read about your past."

"That's sweet," I answered, sliding my hand up her spine and bringing her lips to mine. I kissed her, gently at first. "But this isn't my past."

She kissed me back, a little more fiercely than I had kissed her. "But Hope is part of your past, and this is her story."

"Maybe," I answered, and our kissing became a little more passionate. My hand moved from her back to her soft, perky breasts. She moaned, and my lips abandoned her mouth and settled over her nipples. I could smell her skin, taste her fragrance, and the way she moved her ass over my erection reminded me of just how much I had almost lost in Miami.

And for the first time, I was grateful that Hope hadn't let me make the biggest mistake of my life. That when she chose Matt, she had been looking out for my best interests as well.

"Make love to me, Cam," Riley breathed, holding my face against her chest. "Fuck me hard."

And just like that, our life seemed to have returned to that exact same place where we had lost it.

PRESENT DAY

CHAPTER 51

4:45 PM

Back at the Yacht Club, I thank Josh for his help today. While I carry on a quick and light-hearted conversation with him about my impending unemployment, I notice that Hope and Gordo have started walking toward the Tesla. Unable to trust their conversation, I finish up with Josh and hurry off.

"Hey, Cam!" Josh calls after me.

I glance back at him and notice the big smile on his face.

"Good luck."

Waving my appreciation, I continue after Gordo and Hope. I reach them a few feet from the car, sliding into position next to Hope. Their chat fades into silence.

"Hope I'm not interrupting anything," I blurt.

More silence.

At the Tesla, Gordo fiddles with his iPhone, and the door handles pop out. But before he pulls on his to get inside, he throws me an upward nod and asks where he's taking us next. "The day is almost over, Cam."

Hope slides into the passenger seat and shuts her door, not all that interested in hearing where our conversation will lead or how it will end.

Gordo laughs, shaking his head at me. He pats the roof of the car that nearly ended his marriage three years ago.

"Such an optimist, Gordo," I tell him, sighing.

"You don't really think she's going to miss her flight next week, do you?" he asks me, his eyebrows tightening toward the bridge of his nose.

"She's mine." But I'm not so sure about my own words.

"No," he says, shaking his head with a condescending grin on his face. "In fact, she's not yours, Cam. She's her own woman. Maybe that's why you're setting yourself up for failure." He reaches down for the door handle. "I'm not sticking around, wherever it is that I'm dropping you two off. I'm done. And next week, once she gets on that plane and you're stuck at home with nothing but a Visa bill that you can't pay because your over-schooled ass got greedy for some sour derivative positions…" He shakes his head again, the disgust obvious. "You're on your own, Cam. You know Riley doesn't deserve this."

"You're right," I say, my voice tightening into a narrow hiss. "Riley doesn't deserve this. She doesn't. But neither do I. And until I'm with Hope, the real Cam, the real *me* doesn't exist. What's so hard to understand about that?"

He points at me, annoyed. "You really don't know how stupid you are, do you?" He shakes his head. "I hope Riley never comes back, that she doesn't give you a second—no, a *third* chance.

That girl is a fucking angel, and you're doing this. It's pathetic, a shame."

"I have nothing to say to that, except you're right. Riley won't come back to me. And that's probably why she left. She knows. And she's done sharing."

He chuckles. "Yeah. Sharing you with someone who doesn't want you. Smart move." He opens his door, indicating the end to our conversation.

I glance back toward Josh's boat and see him sweeping the deck, tidying up like he can't afford to pay someone to do that kind of grunt work for him. I feel alone in this moment, my heart beating a mile a minute as I reach down and open the rear passenger side door. Sliding into the cool cabin, I refuse to look in the mirror where I know I'll find Gordon's prying glare.

"Where to, Cam?" he asks, point-blank.

Staring out the window, I remember that split-decision moment when I returned home to Riley after my trip to Miami three years ago. I wonder how my life would look today had I taken a different approach, namely the one that involved apologizing rather than asking for Riley's forgiveness. If I had decided to chase Hope back then, I would not be mentally preparing myself for these two things in my imminent future: the goodbye Hope has never said to me and the divorce papers that Riley will inevitably send.

"Cam, are you awake back there?" He taps the steering wheel in impatience.

Without moving my attention from the window, I rely on my

mistakes from three years ago to give everyone else what they want.

"The train station," I say. "It's getting late. Hope needs to get home."

HIGH SCHOOL

CHAPTER 52

The summer before college, I came to two interesting conclusions about myself. The first was I would never love anyone quite as much as I loved Hope McManus. The second happened somewhere between the blowjob in the front seat of my father's Jeep Grand Cherokee and the crème brulee dessert at Olive Garden, where we decided to share our last meal as an uneducated couple. For us, this was a nice dinner because it wasn't fast food.

"You're pretty calm about all of this," I told her, feeding her a chunk of the dessert's hard surface layer. The way she took my spoon into her mouth and closed her eyes made me want her again. She had a magical way about her, a way that made the rest of the world around us disappear. Whenever we were together, all I saw was Hope and her beauty.

"You belong to me," she said once she swallowed what was in her mouth, grabbing my hand and giving it a firm squeeze. With her other hand, she stroked each of my fingers, leaving a numbing tingle in the wake of each pass.

Hope raised her attention, locking her eyes on mine. Despite all of her confidence, I saw her insecurities; I had spent most of our high school career loving each one of them and proving to her that they made me love her even more fiercely than I had before she shared them with me.

"And you belong to me," I replied, my throat a little tight. Damn, she hid those insecurities a lot better than I could.

"Don't forget it, Cameron." She released my hand and quickly claimed the spoon, scooping the last of the crème brulee into her mouth.

"Goob!" I said, maybe a little too loudly, but her evil laughter eclipsed whatever disruption my name-calling may have caused.

After paying the bill, we left the restaurant with my arm around her waist and hers around me. The older couples we passed in the front waiting area smiled at us like I was the high school quarterback with the lead cheerleader on his arm. We were no such thing.

"I love you, Cameron," she said, giggling. "And someday, you'll be my husband."

I kissed the side of her head. "That day won't come soon enough."

"Five years isn't a long time." She rolled her eyes at me.

"Long enough."

I opened the Grand Cherokee's passenger door, but before she climbed up into the cabin, she hooked her fingers into the waist of my pants and put that lost-looking smile on her lips.

"Kiss me, Cameron," she whispered.

I obeyed her. I could never say no to Hope, it wasn't worth it. As our tongues danced, I felt her fingers running through my hair, but they may as well have been running through my soul. I knew there would never be a replacement for this girl.

"I think you're my air, too," she panted, the first to pull away. Her eyes opened slowly, and her love-drunk glaze told me everything I needed to know—she would never find a replacement for me either.

"You can't steal that," I warned her with a playful grin. "The air thing, that's all mine."

"Shut up, goob. You stole that from someone, and you know it."

I grinned. "Nope."

"You're a fucking plagiarist," she accused me, punching me lightly in the abdomen before climbing inside and shutting the passenger door with a light-hearted eye roll.

"I don't know about this five-year plan, Hope," I said, hesitating as I settled behind the steering wheel and pulled my seatbelt across my lap.

She stared into her lap, fidgeting with her fingers. "It's a promise, not a plan." Her voice came out so quietly; she had to repeat the words.

"And promises aren't made to be broken, right?"

"Broken promises are called lies," she answered without missing a beat.

I drove her home in silence, the mountains dark against the pale, night sky. While many of our friends were out partying during their last weekend before moving into their college dorms next week, Hope and I had opted for this "last dinner" together. In fact, our entire summer vacation had been spent together, drinking in every possible minute together because we both knew how difficult the absence would be.

At her parents' house, I parked on the street and killed the engine. The lights were blazing in every window on the main level, but then again it was only eight PM, not midnight. Plus, it was Friday; even my ancient parents lasted later than midnight on a Friday night.

"What are you going to do now?" Hope asked.

"Still have some packing." I chuckled, because it wasn't the packing I feared. "Why do airlines book flights so fucking early?" I shook my head. I feared the silence, the moments where I could think about the next five years without her in my life. Packing was a fucking breeze.

"I won't cry, Cameron," she promised.

"I know." Now it was my turn to look into my lap. "You sure you'll be there?"

"Yes." She touched my face, closing her eyes like she wanted to memorize every angle, ever corner the way a blind person might. "I would never forgive myself if I missed saying goodbye."

"Then don't," I blurted. Five years was a long time, especially when we only had four years of school ahead of us.

She raised an eyebrow.

"Come with me. Fly to Chicago, let's see the city together, let's spend the weekend in jazz clubs and making fun of the freshwater beaches. And the cold weather. Fuck it, Hope, come with me. I'll get a job, I'll—"

She kissed me to silence me. "It's okay, we'll get through this."

"So you're coming with me?"

She laughed, shaking her head. "Maybe you should come with me, Cameron. I've got the higher earning potential as a chartered accountant. Plus, I'm not flying out until Tuesday, so we'd have more time together here." She winked at me. "Just saying."

My gut told me to take that offer, to run away with her because she was right. She was always right. And knowing my own personal work ethic this past year, despite the straight A's and respectable GPA, the idea of skipping out on school wasn't entirely foreign to me. Nothing else would please me as much as spending my entire days with and for Hope.

"Let's not turn this into a night of tears and sadness, Cameron. Come open my door and hug me one last time so I can dream about you tonight, so I can wake up tomorrow morning and meet you at the airport at four-thirty to say one more goodbye before I see you again at Christmas."

I searched her eyes for some kind of fault line in that solid determination of hers. I saw none. *Okay. Okay, I can do this.*

I got out of my parents' SUV and opened Hope's door for her. She fell straight into my arms and held me tighter than anyone else ever had or ever would again. And it felt perfect, too. Because I wasn't so sure she would make it to the airport the next morning.

PRESENT DAY

CHAPTER 53

5:15 PM

Gordon stops the Tesla outside Ogilvie Transportation Center. Masses of people pour into the building, eager to get home for the Labor Day weekend after a long Friday at the office. It surprises to me to see how few people called in sick today, like I did.

"It was a pleasure seeing you again, Hope," Gordon says, extending his hand to her. It seems like it's a half-goodbye and half-peace offering. "Safe travels and good luck." That part sounded like "good riddance" to me.

Hope shakes his hand and thanks him for the wishes, which sounds like "fuck you, too" to me. And then she glances into the backseat, her face as fierce and determined as ever. "Take care, Cameron." But I know better. I know Hope. I've drunk her in for my entire life. She's my sustenance, and I know that fierce and determined is masking something softer.

I open my door in response; it feels like the right thing to do after such a long day of running up against a door that never opened. "I'll wait for the train with you. I think you'll miss the three-four-seven, so we'll have at least fifteen minutes before the three-four-nine." I allow a beat before adding, "One last goodbye." Then I step out of the Tesla without looking back.

Within seconds, Hope joins me, standing so close I can feel the energy radiating off her body.

"I told you this wasn't a good idea, Cameron," she tells me as we walk into the train station. "But you wanted one last day. You got it. Are you happy?"

Nodding in agreement, I squeeze past a couple of people reading the board for their track. "I got what I wanted. And now I just want to say good…" I swallow the lump in my throat. She doesn't press for me to finish the word, so I let it go.

We stroll deeper into the train station, heading toward the escalators that will bring us to the tracks, then Hope steers off course and sits on a bench against the wall. I walk over to her and sit down as well.

"What was this?" she asks for the millionth time, and her voice comes out in one exhausted breath. "Cameron, you said you'd let me go, but you said you'd never quit, you'd never let go, and I don't know what to believe after today."

"I don't know—"

"It was nice, by the way." She gives my knee an encouraging, friendly pat. "Everything you did, it was magical, it was the Disney of big people, the fairy tale I never got as a child. The way you transformed those parts from *Our Story*, brought them to life for me. Half of the time today, I wondered if you and Emma were somehow conspiring against me." She laughs at her own comments. "Anyway, it was sweet of you to recreate that, to give me this last goodbye."

"You really believe that shit, don't you?"

"What shit, goob?" She punches my shoulder, harder than any prior assault.

"That goodbyes are forever?"

Hanging her head, she allows a depressing nod. "When Emma shared her story with me, the one her so-called 'soul mate' wrote for her, I thought you were that guy. Oliver was one hundred percent you, Cameron. Everything from his profession to his choice of espresso bar. There was so much of you, of *us* in there, it was so obvious to me that you had created this story and given it to Emma to share with me."

I shake my head, chuckling at a part of my past that would always belong there. "I'm sorry, I don't know anyone named Emma. A Katja, yes, but definitely no Emmas." I chuckle again. "And as for the writing, I haven't written anything outside of analysis reports in well over a decade."

"I know," she admits, rolling her eyes and staring up at the tall ceiling. "In a weird twist of fate, I ended up meeting the guy who wrote *Our Story*; his company worked with my firm at the time. Anyway, when Emma gave me the short novel I shared with you, three years ago? I almost died after reading it."

We watch the people hurrying to their trains. The clock rolls past 5:35, and then I feel her hand slide into mine. When I glance over at her, I find something she kept hidden from me all day today.

Hope.

Herself.

I want to hold her like I held her two months ago when she came back to my apartment, like I did three years ago in Miami, and that weekend in her hotel room. More than anything, I just want to be *with* her, close to her. Close enough that we can hold hands, and I don't have to second-guess what she's thinking and feeling. I want Hope because anything less is not life. Without her, I'm not living; I merely exist.

"You missed the three-four-nine," I point out, bringing her hand to my lips and kissing each of her knuckles. I don't even care if she stays; I'm in love with this instant, this moment.

"I know." She laughs, then lowers her voice to a whisper as she plants her head on my shoulder. "I might miss the next one, too."

Eight minutes later, she misses the 351 just like she suggested, but I don't brag about it because this is my time, *our* time. I glance at her, though. And I see her perfect smile before she asks a question I never expected from her today.

"Why did you marry her, Cameron? Can you tell me?"

COLLEGE FRESHMAN YEAR

CHAPTER 54

The airport felt abandoned at this time of morning, with only a few other people present. No one else from my high school had decided to go to Northwestern. Then again, I was that guy who was always spending time with his girlfriend. My friendships could've been deeper, but it would've meant sacrificing what none of the others would ever know—Hope's love.

My parents embraced me, my mother cried. I searched the airport for signs of Hope, but I didn't see her. I figured she had slept in, and I never questioned that she wanted to hurt me by not coming to say goodbye. I never questioned any of her motives back then because I had no reason.

"You should get through security," my father told me, giving me a gentle nudge. "Safe travels."

I started toward the checkpoint and chanced one more glance down the length of the airport. Nothing.

When I checked on my parents, I saw that they were walking away as well. That moment was the loneliest, darkest, and scariest I had ever known. For the first time ever, I felt like Hope had abandoned me, right there at the airport. And all that lay ahead of me was, well…life. And that life was lonely, dark, and scary.

But then—

"Cameron!"

I turned around and in a scene straight out of a romance movie, Hope ran into my arms, leaping up and allowing me to catch her while she buried her face and wrapped her legs around me. She called it a spider-monkey, the way she leaped into the air and used all of her limbs to seize me with the promise of never letting go. I couldn't help but smile, a stupid big grin like we were being reunited rather than saying goodbye.

"I'm sorry I'm late," she sobbed, her tears soaking through my jacket.

"You said you weren't going to cry."

"Then don't look at me, goob!" a watery laugh escaped her grinning lips.

"I'm not. But I can still hear it in your voice."

She laughed and eventually released me.

"I already miss you," I said quietly.

"I already miss you morether."

Huh? "That's not a word, Hope."

Hope shrugged and accused me of not "getting it." She reached out and took my hand, her face breaking up again, the tears pooling in her hazel eyes—*I'll miss those fucking eyes.* "My life without you, Cameron? It's not worth breathing."

"Nah, don't say that," I told her, trying to lighten the mood.

She gave me an elaborate nod, then pressed her hand to my

chest. "It's true. But even without you in my everyday, I'll know that each breath I take will bring us closer. So I won't stop living, because 'closer' is better than never."

"I breathe for you, too."

"I know," she admitted, looking back up to my face with those heartbroken eyes. "And if you stop, I'll know because it'll break me. Don't break me, Cameron."

I chuckled. "How could I ever stop? I love you more than air."

We kissed and she pulled away, starting to take backward steps, but I grabbed her wrist and yanked her back.

"I love you, Hope."

"I can't wait for Christmas, you know that, right? To hold you and be held by you again. And that's when I'll say 'I love you' again."

"Then Christmas break can't come quickly enough, can it?" I asked, squeezing her a little tighter.

She shook her head. "It can't." She squared her shoulders and nodded past me at the TSA security checkpoint. "You better not miss that flight."

I held on to her hand a little longer, just long enough to memorize the feeling. And when I released her, she gave a final smile before turning and walking away.

"Goodbye, Hope."

She didn't glance back; she just kept walking, keeping her chin up and raising a hand to indicate that she had heard me. But she never said it, never said goodbye.

CHAPTER 55

The Chicago snow impressed me. I had never known that cold temperatures could literally cause pain, but the cold here had left me aching. It was very different from the ache I had felt for the past three months while missing Hope; this climactic ache was something I could survive fairly easily by turning up the heat or cocooning myself in a thick comforter.

I cancelled my flight home for Christmas break back in November. I hadn't heard from Hope since the end of October. Part of that reason could've been my fault for not responding to some of her crazy emails and phone calls, but to see how easily she could continue without contacting me…it hurt.

The cold also made me lonely. Ever since the snow started, I missed more class than I had in my entire high school career.

"Merry Christmas, Cam," someone said, poking their head into the dorm room and hurrying off. The stranger was all dressed up in a heavy jacket, scarf, and the kind of hat that gangsters wore.

I gave a silent wave and returned to some of the assigned reading we had been given for the holiday break. I was a couple of hours into reading a few chapters and marking up the text with a highlighter when I heard the brush of paper along the floor. I got up from the bed and walked to the door, noticing the envelope.

Mail?

I flipped it over. The return address belonged to Hope McManus's parents'. Despite the implications, I tore the envelope open and found a single page.

i believe

i believe you live once and that better opportunities are lost on second chances.

i believe true love is about as real as Santa Claus, but 'tis the season, so let's play this game...

i believe that you fall in "love" with the person who lets you love him or her the way you want, on your terms.

i believe if someone says he "loves" you more than air, he's lying to you.

i believe that "love" is not about forgiveness, it's about acceptance, and acceptance keeps relationships alive.

i believe in the stories that are never told.

i believe that if you have to "fight" for love, you're trying to force a square peg into a round hole.

i believe that your flaws are what make you beautiful. Deal with it.

i believe that two people are just that—two people.

i believe that two married people are two individuals with one shared goal and one shared delusion.

i believe delusions are a good thing until you start getting drugs, threesomes, and whips involved. Stay pure.

i believe that in your heart, you have blood not love, and that blood is to the heart what ideas (not love) are to the mind.

i believe that happy endings happen in real life when I fall asleep, thinking of my children's smiles.

i believe that all stories are written for me—that same story means something different for you, and that's okay.

i believe in freedom for everyone; everyone has the right to hunt or to hide, or both.

i believe that mothers are sacred and anyone who tells a mother what to do has self-esteem issues.

i believe that true character gets revealed in actions, not in what someone says about him or herself.

i believe that promises are one word, and any one word means nothing.

i believe that if you never hurt, you never find happiness; the bigger you hurt, the bigger your happiness.

i believe in friendships that last a lifetime and in friends that support you even when you are dead wrong.

i believe that most of the decisions you make are the wrong ones. Celebrate your victories. Celebrate hard.

i believe that if you can make decisions objectively, you will never be wrong. Or hurt. Or happy.

i believe that we cry for ourselves, not for others.

i believe that tears are a lot like rage—you need to get that poison out of your system periodically or it will kill you.

i believe that when you die, you die alone, and

i believe that goodbyes are forever.

I had to read the poem several times over. I knew it had broken her heart to put all these words on paper, but the only line that really mattered was the last one. I memorized as much as I could, afraid to fold this last piece of her away and get on with whatever waited for me on the other side of Hope McManus.

Because I now believed that goodbyes are forever, too. And goodbye was the last thing I had said to her before flying to Chicago.

CHAPTER 56

That night, with the dorm mostly empty, I left campus and walked a few blocks to a small sushi restaurant in a plaza that a few of the others in the dorm had talked about. It was a new restaurant, and the fish had a reputation for being fresh. Plus, the booths offered a bit of privacy, which was what I wanted. And not what I got. Instead, the table where the hostess seated me was at the window, allowing me a view of the parking lot. Not exactly scenic, but I didn't care. I wanted to eat and re-read the poem Hope had sent. The place was pretty quiet with students being away. I wanted to figure out the rest of my life, wanted some silence and a nice raw fish dinner.

At least, it started out that way, but roughly midway through my dragon rolls, I noticed a blonde walking past my window—the prettiest scenery all evening. She wore a black fabric jacket that stretched halfway down her thighs with a wide, fashionable collar. Her skirt with black tights had me wondering whether she wore anything underneath that jacket.

Of course, she caught me gawking at her perfectly sculpted legs. She stopped and faced me, placing her hands on her hips, while simultaneously shooting me a disgusted glare that had her face all twisted up.

I raised my hands in an apology, mouthing '*Not what it looks like*,' but she rolled her eyes and kept walking to the convenience store next door.

Shoving another roll into my mouth, I tried to forget how I had just embarrassed myself. And it worked, for the most part—aided by some wasabi that hit my tongue at the wrong angle—but I couldn't forget her face, her pale blonde hair that fell over her shoulders in long, wavy strokes. And of course those eyes, their vibrancy, and the way they looked vulnerable and all-knowing at the same time.

I was still staring out the window, chewing on my meal when the blonde walked by again, her eyes digging into me with enough energy that I couldn't help but look up and meet her stare. She reached into her jacket and opened a pack of cigarettes, which she had clearly just purchased. Pressing a cigarette between her lips, she watched me as she lit up and sucked in a few deep breaths.

And then she started coughing, eventually losing her shit, leaning forward on her knees like she might get sick or pass out. Then she spit the cigarette on the ground. She crushed it with her boot, and when she raised her attention to me again, I started laughing.

She smiled as well, the first sign that she had forgiven me for gawking at her legs earlier. I gave a mild wave before returning to my meal, and I noticed her walking away in my peripheral vision. The first thought I had was, *I fucking miss Hope.*

But before I could think on it for too long, I heard those boots strutting up to my window table. I tried to ignore her, but her perfume sailed to me like the salt off the ocean breeze, barely present, yet I knew it was there. And if that wasn't enough, her blonde hair seemed to glow in the reflection of the glass.

"You're not a smoker," I stated the obvious, keeping my face buried in the sushi so she couldn't see the smile she had aroused, a smile that should not have existed without Hope's presence.

"You're not a perv," she answered.

I chuckled quietly, well aware that sometimes it was best to stay silent rather than risk ruining a good thing.

"Can I sit?"

I nodded. "I'd like that."

As she slid into the booth across from me, she opened her black jacket to reveal the white blouse underneath. It looked formal, very nice.

"You're right," I told her. "I'm not a perv."

She giggled and looked good doing it. "And I'm not a smoker."

"I'm Cam."

"I'm Riley."

We laughed. My appetite waned after that single conversation, and I realized the meal I had ordered was far too ambitious for me. I offered her a roll, and when she gave me an affirmative nod, I fed it to her with the chopsticks. I had never fed a stranger before, but something about Riley felt familiar, maybe it was the smile that erased all of the bad in the world. She was a new beginning.

That was how I met Riley, the woman with hair so blonde you swore she was Heaven's equivalent to a Wal-Mart greeter, and legs so fine the only thing you could imagine was what they would feel like wrapped around you, around your neck.

Just like that, Hope fell into a compartment of my mind that I could forget about, the one that allowed me to try and accept that goodbyes were indeed forever.

I never asked why Riley wanted to take up smoking that night, and she never brought it up.

PRESENT DAY

CHAPTER 57

8:01 PM

Stepping into my condo, I notice that Riley must've come by to collect some of her things. Why she needed the Keurig, microwave, and a few other things will forever be a mystery, but something I know she doesn't need is, well, me. We still own the executive townhouse in the suburbs, and I suspect that's where she will end up moving after giving the tenants the required noticed to terminate their lease.

I walk through the kitchen and head straight to the Bat Cave, closing the sliding French doors for that extra layer of isolation. It surprises me that she didn't defecate or otherwise ruin this room. Then again, Riley's a classy woman. Hope was right about her—she never deserved any of this.

Despite my utter lack of motivation after watching Hope board the 361 Metra that left the Ovie at 7:35, I reach for the keyboard and access the internet on the large television. I notice that Landon has sent a margin call on the futures contract I booked through his firm. It's an obligation I will fail to fulfill.

Officially, I've lost everything.

I check the email account and see the messages from Raj, which I could just as easily access through my phone. Instead, I read the big words on the screen:

> **Raj:** Newman has evidence that you're not sick. I've been instructed to terminate you, Cam. I'm sorry.

Correction from earlier: *Now* I've officially lost everything.

I toss the wireless keyboard onto the floor and lay back into Topsy when I hear the knock at the door. My first thought drifts to Hope, but I remember seeing the train leave the station.

Hopping out of the beanbag, I hurry to the door and open it—to Newman. The smile on his face makes my wasted sick day feel utterly tragic. When he hands me an envelope and clears his throat, I worry that the excitement might nudge him into cardiac arrest.

"Hope it was worth it," he tells me.

Funny choice of words. "Hope is worth it, yes."

My response confuses him, so he shrugs it off. "It gave me great pleasure to find you outside the Walgreen's on North Michigan today, Cam. That's all I needed. And Rick in IT was able to see how you manipulated the employee system to make it look like you still had sick days." He taps the side of his head. "Might not have the best memory, but I've been watching you all year, motherfucker."

"That's sweet, Newman. But you know something? Shit happens for a reason. And terminating me gives me a reason."

More of that deer-in-the-headlights look.

I reach for the door to close it, but give my worst-boss-ever a final glance. "Are we done here?"

He stumbles on his words. "I…that…the, uh, payout is just the minimum, asshole. State regs."

I give him a thankful grin because if he had evidence to terminate my employment with cause, he really didn't have to fund any kind of payout. It was nice that he had, though. It might cover my flight to chase down Hope.

"Goodnight, Newman." I start shutting the door, but his foot stops me. Sighing, I open up for him. Again.

"You did great work, Cam," he admits with a reluctant pity. "It's just too bad you're such a fucking idiot. I hated your face, your attitude, just everything about you."

I don't think we will miss each other, Newman and I. "Is this goodbye?"

But he's already walking away.

Closing the door, I don't bother to make sure he gets on the elevator. I open the envelope and see a single check from Second City Financial. It's more substantial than I figured it would be—enough to cover the margin call, anyway.

And maybe a standby airline ticket.

CHAPTER 58

10:21 PM

I hear another knock a couple of hours later, interrupting the game on the television. My face burns from the wine I drank—the Ontario wine that Riley and I had discovered so long ago. When I stand up, I feel a little lightheaded. Not drunk, but also in no condition to operate a motorized vehicle.

Walking toward the door, I wonder if it might be Newman again. Or Riley, but she has a key and would undoubtedly let herself in. My last hope is that it's, well, Hope.

As I reach for the door handle, I notice my rapid heartbeat, the anticipation and sense of optimism. It's her…I just know it.

I can literally feel Hope's familiar presence, and it's got my entire spirit trembling. Before I latch onto the door handle, I take a deep breath. And for the first the time since the night I first saw Riley outside that long-forgotten sushi restaurant, I understand why she could never take up smoking. It wasn't natural. Not like this, not like how the essence of Hope belongs with me.

With a hesitation that I blame on just how horribly my day has gone, I turn the knob and open the door, but I'm staring down at my feet. No, I'm not staring—my eyes are closed, sealed shut because I don't want to open them to anyone else but Hope.

And then I feel her hand on my face, her soft fingertips leaving a tingle in their wake. Her touch robs my fears, replaces them with a warmth I can only describe as pure love.

"Open your eyes," I hear her whisper. "It's okay. You can open them now."

I shake my head. I was wrong about so many things today—wrong about Hope, wrong about *Our Story*, wrong about getting away with my sick day at work. I was wrong about Newman, wrong about Gordo, wrong about…*everything.*

"I don't want to be wrong anymore," I whisper.

"Cameron," she says. And in my heart and soul and entire being, I know it's her—I know it's Hope—but I just can't bring myself to look and see for myself. "You need to open your eyes now."

I shake my head a little more fiercely.

So she kisses me, and those lips confirm everything—the feel, the taste, the warmth.

It's Hope. My Hope.

"Open your eyes, goob! If you want to know how *Our Story* really ends, look at me and let me tell you my four words. Let me tell you what I've never been able to say to you."

Goodbye?

She sighs, but continues to hold my face with her hands. Then she brings her forehead to mine, and we're so close, I can feel the honesty in what she tells me. "I love you, Cameron."

"My four words," I whisper, my chest threatening to burst. "I love you, Hope."

I lean in for another kiss, but she cranes her neck away. "No…" she says, her eyes widening. "No, Cameron. Those aren't the four words. The four words are these: I love you more."

At last, I take a deep breath and open my eyes.

Hope is mine.

Forever.

EPILOGUE

While waiting for the doctor to call me into his office for my test results, I stared at the pictures inside a *National Geographic.* I tried to read the article, but my mind wandered, worried about whether Oliver would come home on time tonight. The fear that he wouldn't show up was a recurring one with no merit, but I still worried because our love had been one of struggle, of fighting and perseverance. Now that we had finally come together, I worried.

While the pictures for the article impressed me, I realized that the two loneliest places in the world were the arrivals gate at the airport—mostly when you arrived and nobody greeted you—and a doctor's office after you were called in to discuss test results. Even if Oliver had joined me, this would feel like the loneliest moment of my day.

"Ms. Warren?" one of the administrators said. "This way, please." She ushered me through the tight halls to the wood-paneled office at the end. Volumes of medical texts lined the shelves on one of those walls, and I wondered if Dr. Reynolds had indeed read every one of them. I sat in a chair and was told "the doctor" would arrive shortly.

Half an hour later, he entered the office, whistling and carrying a folder with my test results inside. He sat behind his nice desk, read the remarks, and the whistling ended with an *oh shit* finality.

He looked up at me, and I could tell he barely recognized me from when I first approached him six months or so ago when we first started this process of tests—the blood tests first, then the specialist, then the CT scan, then the MRI.

It was bad news. And while he told me to get my affairs in order, all I could think about was how Oliver would so easily survive without me.

It didn't take all that long for my condition to get worse. And when things got to the point where I couldn't manage while Oliver was at work, I insisted that he bring me to the hospital. We both knew I would never come home, and while that decision broke my heart it wrecked Oliver worse. Over the course of these past few months, he had aged, a lot. Because love does that—it wrecks you.

"Wait," I said at the door to our small apartment. I kicked my shoes off, smiling at the memory of that first night we had spent together, entering that room and kicking my shoes off way back then. "I want to say goodbye to our home."

He gave me a pleasant smile, then caught up to me as I entered our bedroom. Together, we stared at the bed where we had made the most memorable love of my life. Sliding his arm around my waist, he kissed the side of my face and told me he loved me.

"I love you, too," I replied, and then walked to the bathroom where we had also made love, where he had proposed to me while I applied eye goop to my face. I toyed with my wedding ring, and Oliver knew where my memory had taken me. That day. That proposal.

"I'm so happy we're married, Olivia," he confessed, his face suddenly younger as he remembered that morning.

"We fought hard for that, didn't we?" I squeezed his arm.

"Nobody has ever fought as hard for anything as you fought for our love."

I gave him a playful jab to the ribs. "I've still got some fight in me, goob."

He chuckled and tried to lead me away from the bathroom, but I stayed planted in the room.

"The bullshit we put each other through, Oliver…" I shook my head.

"Shhh," he said. He kissed me next, probably to keep me quiet, to keep the tears at bay. "We have each other now."

I shook my head again and ran my hand along the bathroom counter. I had spent tears there, worried about losing the life we had finally captured, the life of togetherness. Refusing to shed another tear on a past I could never change, I stepped away from the bathroom and peeked into the second bedroom.

The kids we would never have could've lived in that room. But even without this sickness robbing me of precious days with each breath, we were too old for kids once we were together. That bothered me a little, but Oliver said he didn't want to share me with anyone. I liked that. Now, though, staring at the sofa bed and second television in this room, I wished we had gotten our act together sooner. Because knowing that Oliver had a lot of living left in him, and he would never find another companion to replace me, trusting our child to take care of him and check in on him on those special occasions would've provided me with an extra layer of comfort.

He had nothing now. His own children would visit once they were bored, but they would never take the initiative to visit the man who had crushed their mother's heart. He would be alone once I was gone.

"I hate this room," he told me, looking back down the hall where all the good memories were.

I chuckled. "What will you do with it once I'm…you know?"

He walked away.

I followed him to the living room, stared out the balcony windows at the city outside. We had enjoyed wine, laughter, and conversations on that balcony, even as recently as last week when all I could do was smile at him and think, *I will absolutely miss every breathing moment with this man.*

"I'm going to move into a house," Oliver declared. "I don't think I'll be able to sleep here tonight, let alone once you're…you know."

"How will you watch the stars, then?" I asked.

"I'll make sure I have a big patio, and I'll watch for you from there. I don't need this balcony."

We had decided in bed some time ago, when the medication stopped working the way it should, that once I died, I would speak to him through shooting stars. There had been some argument about the anniversary of our first kiss, but Oliver had eventually agreed on April fourth. It really could've been June twentieth or July twenty-first or even August twenty-second. I couldn't remember because that day we spent together and kissed for the first time was a day spent in absolute Heaven. And I would speak to him through the shooting stars *every* day.

Love can do that. It's fierce. It's permanent. It outlives our bodies, and it outlives *us.*

I awoke in the hospital a little later, not sure what had happened. Oliver hurried over the moment he saw that my eyes were open and, when I tried to speak, nothing came out but a whisper.

"I'm here, Olivia," he said, his eyes tearing up.

"Don't be a pussy," I scolded him.

He chuckled, then kissed me hard because that was how much he loved me. He loved me with the hard permanence of forever.

"I want our wedding picture," I told him.

He hurried away and rummaged through a bag, surprising me when he produced the exact photo I requested.

He winked at me. "Soul mates."

I stared at the photo of this handsome man I had spent the best years of my life chasing and loving, and I smiled to myself before pressing the frame to my chest and closing my eyes. I knew I would die staring at Oliver's face, either the real version hovering over me at this moment, or the photographed version that I held to my chest.

And dying like that—with the last image you see being the man that you love…a happy ending despite the absence of a happily ever after…I…Hope—I hope for that kind of death. No, for that kind of *life* for everyone.

THE END

acKNOWLEDGMENts

My wife, Ms. Parker, without your support and critical eye, my dream of becoming an author would never be realized. Ever. Thank you for tolerating everyone else and allowing me to be the only normal person in this world.

Amy Clark, you're a lot like my work-wife. You nag and push and are the most persistent UKer I know. More reliable than a Renault Robin, although you're equally easy to tip over. Anyway, any and all success is attributable to you, your hard work and your bizarre commitment to this Morgan Parker Project of ours. Thank you for making me look better that I ever could be.

Megan Hand thank you for your high-level story advice and keen eye for details. You helped me fall in love with this story that I've written, and I'm forever indebted to you.

Madison Seidler, thank you for your keen eye and for going easy on me. You played a difficult role with this novel and I'm very thankful to have met someone as patient and detailed as you are. Thank you for not making me cry.

The Top-Secret Morganettes – MJ F, you've been there from day 1 and stuck with my stories even through the really bad ones… I can't thank you enough for being the "one person" who made the "one difference" that everyone underestimates; D T, you've inspired me from the moment I published my first story, I don't understand why, but you still do and I love you for that; Kelsey B, your tough-love approach doesn't really work but without it I wouldn't keep reaching and stretching for something better, each time; Shell B, your humor and energy make me tired… thank you for teaching me about true risks; Rhonda K who is my living proof that real-life love stories really do exist; Laveda K, your skill at getting under my skin while simultaneously making me feel like the most talented person alive is uncanny (and sweet); Helen, for ongoing humor and especially for brining Sick Day alive with your amazing talent for finding the right images for the right teasers; Jenny Z, for your liveliness, energetic attitude and all of the kind words you've had for my stories and writing; Pamela M, for your tireless efforts in bringing life to this brand known as Morgan Parker, I can't thank you enough; Janett G, for believing in me enough that you've shared me with "real life" people who are old enough to know better than read my kind of novels, and for sharing those stories with the group and proving that my stories *can* be enjoyed at any age; Amy L, you remind me of where I want to be, which is a place called Happy, and; Patricia G, for your constructive feedback and criticism which is a fancy way of saying, thank you for pushing me to want and to do better. Thank you, ladies, for allowing me to be myself without consequences, and for letting me into your lives <3

I have so many supporters I would love to thank individually. You know who you are. You. You are my readers and cheerleaders, the ones who, like me, don't see their name in print but without whom this novel would never have made a single sale (no, really, even my mom couldn't have bailed me out here because she doesn't have Kindle). So yes, you!

Thank you.

ABOUT MORGAN PARKER

Morgan Parker is the pen name of a shy and introverted male author. When he's not writing, he enjoys spending time with his family, outdoors or engaged in some kind of physical activity that will get the kids to bed early enough that he can have an uninterrupted chat with his wife.

Morgan splits his time between Toronto, Ontario, Canada and the worlds inside his head. As the author of *Hope, non friction*, and the *Textual Encounters* series, he believes that the best stories are the ones that are never told. So he's working hard at telling them.

Follow Morgan Parker on Facebook and Twitter to learn more about the different stories he plans on sharing with you soon!